"Nice boys have fantasies, too."

"Do they?" Simone asked.

"Yes, they do," Chance said, his voice growing husky. "And some boys don't control them that well."

"Is that so?"

"Mmm-hmm," he said. "What about nice girls? Do they have fantasies?"

"Some do," she said with a grin that made his mouth go dry. "But they know better than to feed them."

"What if someone else feeds them?" he asked. "What then?"

She dropped her eyelids the slightest degree, then peered up at him. "What have you got in mind?"

The question almost startled him, but he couldn't let it die. His grin slipped farther across his face. "What makes you think I'm talking about me?"

"That look in your eye . . . and all this talk about fantasies . . ."

"I was talking about 'nice boys,' " he said. "No one ever said that description fit me."

ABOUT THE AUTHOR

Tracy Hughes began writing her first romance novel after graduating from Northeast Louisiana University in 1984. While in graduate school, she finished that book in lieu of her thesis and decided to abandon her pursuit of a master's degree and follow her dream of becoming a writer. She is the award-winning author of nineteen novels, including a mainstream and a historical romance. Tracy recently relocated to Mississippi where she makes her home with her two young daughters.

Books by Tracy Hughes

HARLEQUIN AMERICAN ROMANCE

381–HONORBOUND
410–SECOND CHANCES

HARLEQUIN SUPERROMANCE

304–ABOVE THE CLOUDS
342–JO: CALLOWAY CORNERS, BOOK 2
381–EMERALD WINDOWS
399–WHITE LIES AND ALIBIS

TRACY HUGHES

FATHER KNOWS BEST

Harlequin Books

TORONTO • NEW YORK • LONDON
AMSTERDAM • PARIS • SYDNEY • HAMBURG
STOCKHOLM • ATHENS • TOKYO • MILAN
MADRID • WARSAW • BUDAPEST • AUCKLAND

Published May 1992

ISBN 0-373-16438-6

FATHER KNOWS BEST

Printed in U.S.A.

Chapter One

"Off with her head!" The woman's voice shrilled out of the classroom and reverberated through the high school corridor. "She cheated on Henry and she deserves to die!"

"No, she doesn't," a younger voice returned from across the room. "Henry's just telling lies on her so he can have her beheaded and get her out of the way."

"But why would he do that?" the woman asked.

"Because he knows he can't divorce her," a boy said. "Man, it took *years* to get his divorce from Catherine...and if he got the marriage annulled, that red-haired chick with the black teeth—Elizabeth—she couldn't be his heir anymore."

"So he'd rather just *kill* her?"

"Sounds good to me," the boy said. "My dad says it's cheaper than divorce."

The classroom erupted into waves of giggles, and from the windowsill where he leaned in the corridor waiting for the bell to ring, Chance Avery wondered what on earth that banter was all about. Death and divorce? Beheading? What could it all possibly have to do with history?

Unable to contain his curiosity any longer, he took a tentative step toward the door and peered inside, scanning the young faces for the teacher who wielded so much influence over his sixteen-year-old daughter, to the point that she undermined his own authority.

At once he saw her in the center of the room, standing amidst her students in a long royal gown with a fat white wig on her head. His mental picture of her had been of a matronly type with big hips and kind eyes, but his daughter had neglected to mention that the teacher she so admired and respected looked like a little girl playing dress-up in her mommy's clothes.

He gave in to a curious frown that seemed at odds with the laugh lines crinkling his tanned face. So this was where Jeanie had started making her first—and only—*A*s since she left grade school, he thought critically. So this was where she went for the ludicrous, half-baked advice...the advice that she followed as if it were a decree from Heaven. So this was the woman who wielded royal influence over the sixteen-year-old girl who had been the nucleus of his life since his wife died fourteen years ago. He had to admit that he hadn't expected the teacher to look as out of touch with reality as his daughter was. No wonder she had such asinine ideas, he thought. The room, too, looked more like a rehearsal place for a Shakespearean play than a sophomore-level history class, for the students stood rather than sat, their attention centered on the small, vibrant woman who darted around the room throwing capes and wigs and fake swords into their hands as she shot questions out to them.

The bell rang, and the students began shedding their costumes and tossing them into a box at the front of the room. "Don't forget to read the next chapter by tomorrow," the woman called over the noise. "Tomorrow we'll talk about that red-haired chick with the black teeth."

"Hope she's not as boring as she is ugly," one of the students commented with a grin as he gathered his books.

"She is," the teacher deadpanned. "One love affair after another, a war with her sister, more executions..."

Chance saw the interest in the students' eyes spark to life as possibilities tumbled through their minds, and suddenly, in a light-bulb revelation, he realized that they *had* been talking about history. Henry must have been Henry VIII, and the teacher was dressed as Anne Boleyn. She had brought the scene to life, and as bizarre a way as it was to teach, he had to admit it was interesting.

He stood back and waited as they came out of the room and dispersed in various directions, blending into the after-school flow of teenagers filling the hallway. Finally, when she was alone in the room, he knocked.

Simone Stevens looked up instantly when she heard the knock, her eyes immediately assessing him with startling blue clarity. Her first thought upon seeing the raven-haired man leaning against her doorway, clad in skintight jeans that barely tolerated the strong thighs filling them and a casual pullover sweater that only accented the broad shoulders and well-worked biceps beneath it, was that this was the birthday present her practical-joking little brother had warned her about. A grin livened her eyes, and hiking her skirts, which were much too long for her small frame, she started toward him. "Yes?"

"Miss Stevens?" he asked, his expression sober despite the ridiculous picture she knew she represented. So much for first impressions, she thought. "I'm Chance Avery. Jeanie Avery's father. I need to talk to you."

"Sure," she said, breathing a sigh of relief that her brother hadn't sent him. "Jeanie's father, huh? The dog trainer? I was afraid you were a practical joke."

"What?"

"My brother's been hinting around about sending me a present too big to fit into a box and too virile to resist." She shrugged. "Never mind. You'd have to know him." She pulled off her wig, allowing her sable curls to tumble down her shoulders, further defining the clarity of her eyes. "Sorry about this," she said, sweeping a hand down the costume. "We're studying Henry VIII." As if that explanation satisfied any curiosity he might have had about the costume, she slid up onto her desk. "Typical man, old Henry. The love 'em and leave 'em type. Got bored real easy."

"Typical man?" Chance asked, not hiding his offense.

Simone grinned. "Well, maybe that's unfair of me. I'm sure *you're* nothing like that." Her teasing smile was somewhat infectious, but Chance bristled.

"I didn't really come here to discuss my type," he said. "I came to talk to you about my daughter."

"Jeanie's a great kid," she said. "We have a terrific rapport." She nodded toward one of the desks. "Why don't you sit down?"

"Thanks, I'll stand," he said. "I noticed that most of your students prefer not to use their desks, anyway." He sent a scrutinizing glance around the cluttered room, breathing a derisive, mirthless laugh. "History class sure has changed since I was in school."

She recognized the barb for exactly what it was—for her methods were often questioned by teachers and parents who believed in traditional educational techniques. Jack McCall, her principal, had a file an inch thick, full of petty complaints about her classes.

"I believe in personal involvement in the lessons," she said. "Things sink in a little better when they've acted them out and visualized them. I don't really believe in sitting still and taking notes."

"Yeah, well, that personal involvement is exactly what I wanted to talk to you about," he said. "I happen to think you get a little *too* personally involved. Even to the point of meddling."

"Meddling?" Her spine stiffened, and she slid off the desk, letting her skirt puddle around her feet—feet that, he noted, were encased in white sneakers. "Just what are you referring to, Mr. Avery?"

His eyes had an angry silver hue that pierced into her with shaming intensity. "I'm referring to your encouraging my daughter to be in a rock-and-roll band."

She fought the urge to gasp dramatically and feign shock, but told herself that wouldn't help her case any. "Of course, I encouraged her," she said, completely in the dark about what sin that represented. "You don't know your daughter very well, do you, Mr. Avery?"

The very smugness of her response made his face redden, and he tightened his lips. "As a matter of fact,

Miss Stevens, my daughter and I are very close. Just what are you implying?"

"I'm not implying anything, Mr. Avery. It's just that Jeanie has some problems in school. She's apathetic, but that's just a defense mechanism, because she doesn't quite fit in. I've spent months trying to figure out a way to draw her out of herself."

"Draw her out of herself? You act like she's some shy little thing curled up in a shell. She's not like that at all!"

"Yes, she is," Simone said. "She's withdrawn and disinterested. But a few months ago I heard her sing at an audition for the school play, and I was knocked out by her voice. I thought that was just the niche she needed to start blossoming. Were you aware of her talent?"

The question insulted him, and Chance shifted his weight to his other foot and crossed his arms, those eyes lashing her again. "Of course, I'm aware of it. She got it from her mother."

Simone's eyes lost a bit of their effervescence and she glanced at the floor, remembering Jeanie's mention that her mother had died when she was two. "Well," she said, tempering her voice as she went on, "she didn't get the part in the play because, frankly, she's too shy and inhibited to act."

"So instead you suggested a nice, safe, low-profile alternative like rock music?" His voice was rising with increasing anxiety, and Simone knew that if she were not careful, she would have a bona fide confrontation here. And there was nothing she hated more.

"One more complaint," Mr. McCall had told her last week, *"and I'm taking your file to the school board."*

Clearing her throat and trying to sound conciliatory without being apologetic, she tried to explain her motives. "This isn't the fifties, Mr. Avery. Surely you don't see rock music as something to fear. You probably even listened to it when you were her age."

"I *still* listen to it," he said, bristling again. "I'm not that out of touch. And the merits of rock music have nothing to do with my complaint. My daughter is sixteen."

"Mr. Avery, it's just music! An opportunity came up, and I simply asked Jeanie if she was interested. My little brother has this band...and they needed a singer..."

Chance stepped toward her, his face much too close to hers. Eyes the color of a thunderous sky laced with bolts of lightning threatened her, but those incongruous white lines near his eyes made the intimidation a bit less potent. "Lady, I've worked for years to protect my daughter from situations that I don't think are good for her. Jeanie has no business singing in nightclubs in a band with a bunch of pot-smoking walking hormones with guitars."

"I beg your pardon!" Simone blurted, the professional side of her giving way to the family side that always made her defend her brother. "Brian is not a 'walking hormone,' he doesn't abuse drugs and he isn't going to drag your daughter into any nightclubs!" She stepped back, tried to calm herself, then looked up at him again. "If he wasn't my own brother,

I never would have suggested it. But he's a good kid. He's eighteen years old..."

"She wasn't even allowed to *date* until this year!" Chance cut in. "And the fact that he's your brother doesn't reassure me a whole lot. You're the one standing in a sixteenth-century dress with tennis shoes, don't forget. I'm not that convinced of *your* stability."

Simone snapped up her chin and set her hands on her small hips, dwarfed by the heavy fabric of the gown. "I do what it takes to keep my students interested, Mr. Avery. This town has a fifty-two-percent dropout rate. If my dressing in costumes will help me get just a few of those kids past the point of disillusionment with the education system, then that's what I'll do. If my encouraging them in their talents helps to boost their self-esteem, then I'll do that, too."

"Self-esteem?" he asked. "What are you talking about? Jeanie doesn't have a problem with self-esteem."

"And you claim to be close to her," she volleyed, knowing she shouldn't. "She hardly ever says a word, she doesn't relate well to the other kids her age, she doesn't try very hard in school..."

"All the more reason she shouldn't be thrust up on a stage and expected to perform."

"In my opinion, that's precisely why she should."

Chance's tanned complexion changed to a seering pink as he arched his eyebrows sharply. "Well, your opinion doesn't count in this case. You can tell your brother to find another singer for his band." He started toward the door, but turned back on the threshold. "And I'd appreciate it if you'd keep your nose out of my daughter's life in the future. You stick to teaching, and I'll take care of the parenting. I'd say I've had a little more experience than you have."

Simone started toward him, but almost tripped over the skirt. Struggling to reach the back zipper, she called, "Mr. Avery, please! This isn't about me. It's about Jeanie. Think about *her* feelings before you make a decision!"

Chance pivoted and came back into the room, his hand slamming against the door's casing. "I've already made the decision," he said, "and when it comes to my daughter—"

"When it comes to your daughter you can't be objective," Simone said, squirming and trying harder to free her zipper. Her cheeks burned with stifling heat and she yanked the fabric at her back. "You don't really see her out in the real world," she went on through her teeth. "At home, she's safe and secure, but—"

"What are you doing?" Chance asked suddenly as it occurred to him that she was unzipping her dress.

Simone looked up at him, saw the exasperation on his face. His expression might have been comical, had she not been so flustered herself.

"Trying to get out of this thing." Her face flushed with the effort. "Would you give me a hand, please? It's stuck."

"Why do you have to do it now?"

She slung her hair back out of her face. "Because it's hot, and if I have to fight with parents of my students, I make my points better when I'm not tripping over my skirt!"

She turned her back to him and gestured toward the zipper, and reluctantly, awkwardly, Chance took hold of it. She felt him tug slightly, then harder, then finally he settled one large tentative hand over her rib cage and jerked. The dress fell open, revealing the T-shirt and jeans she wore beneath it. Quickly she stepped out of the dress, turned back to him and watched his eyes grudgingly sweep over her, from the breasts that she knew were too vividly obvious beneath the white T-shirt, to her favorite pair of acid-washed jeans. She recognized the censure in his face, the same kind of disapproval her principal had shown when she wore the Lady Godiva costume the first week of school this year. "What is it now?" she asked, bracing herself.

"You don't look any older than your students," he said, as if that fact disgusted him.

Simone accepted the comment with a cocky smile. "Thanks. You're not so bad yourself."

She noted the defensiveness pass over Chance's face, and she wondered just where such a serious guy had gotten such intriguing laugh lines.

"I didn't mean that as a compliment," he said. "How old are you, anyway? Just out of college?"

"I'm thirty. Today, as a matter of fact," she said. "And yes, they still check my ID when I order wine in restaurants. My mother assures me that someday I'll be grateful."

"And this is how you dress when you're teaching those 'walking hormones'?"

His implication that she was a tease who got high on the yearnings of adolescent boys irked her. "No, Mr. Avery," she shot back. "When I'm not in costume, I dress quite appropriately for what I do. I can't very well wear a three-piece suit under that gown, now, can

I? You know, you seem to have an overactive fascination with those so-called walking hormones."

"It's not fascination," he defended. "It's fear. I was once one of them, myself."

The confession, though delivered as an illustration of his point, endeared him and hinted that there, indeed, was a sense of humor buried under all that paternal pride. A slow grin crawled across Simone's lips. "You mean there was really a time when you weren't wound up as tight as a tin soldier?"

Instead of loosening him up with the question, as she had hoped, she only served to wind him tighter. "It was a long time ago," he said. "Before I had a daughter to think about."

"Parenthood isn't synonymous with stuffed shirt, is it?" she asked.

A flash of something—surprise? pain?—flickered through his eyes. "Do you always counter logic with aggression?" he asked suddenly. "It seems to me when you're backed against the corner, about to lose an argument, you start flinging insults."

"I'm not insulting you," she said calmly. "I was merely making an observation. Surely you've been called a stuffed shirt before."

"No, as a matter of fact, I haven't." He pointed a finger at her, his eyes smoldering as he went on. "You know, making snap judgments like that about me is on the same level as my deciding that you're a flake and can't be reasoned with."

"A flake?" Her own face registered surprise, and he saw the tension cross over it. "I am not a flake. I'm a very competent teacher who happens to work miracles with students who come into my class barely knowing who George Washington was."

"But when *I* first saw you, you looked like a flake. Standing there in that silly wig and shrieking out dialogue about beheading Anne Boleyn..."

"Well, well," she cut in, eyes flashing. "The man knows his history. I would have guessed you'd never heard of her."

"Yeah, seems like I heard something about her when I was riding in on the hay truck yesterday. In my stuffed shirt."

She grinned slightly. "All right. You've made your point. I'm wrong for making a snap judgment. Or at least for articulating it."

"And I shouldn't have called you an airhead," he conceded, a hint of a grin reaching his eyes.

She laughed slightly. "You're an interesting man, Mr. Avery."

"And you're an incorrigible woman," he returned.

For a moment they held each other locked in thoughtful scrutiny. Finally he said, "So much for first impressions, huh?"

She grinned a grin that made her seem even more incorrigible and shrugged. "I don't know. My first impression of you was that you were the virile hunk my brother warned me about."

Slightly taken aback, he gauged her with eyes that held the slightest spark of flirtation. "My first impression of you was that you looked like a kid playing dress-up." He started back to the door, and turned back before stepping into the corridor. "And a flake."

She grinned but didn't respond, for she knew that he no more thought that of her than she thought he was a stuffed shirt.

"Do me a favor and cut out the amateur counseling with my daughter, okay?" he said more seriously. "They have professionals for that sort of thing, assuming she ever needs it. And if all else fails, she can always turn to her father."

"When she quits asking for my advice," she said, "I'll quit giving it."

Once again, that hard look returned to his face. "You're a slow learner, aren't you, Miss Stevens?"

She stiffened, and realized she might have pushed him too far. He wasn't only a man who had just given her the most stimulating bit of banter she had had in weeks, he was the parent of a student. An angry parent. One who could do her a lot of harm, if she didn't placate him.

"Don't worry, Mr. Avery," she said finally. "I won't usurp your parental authority. I hope you'll let her be in the band, but if you don't, I'll leave it alone. It's not my intention to encourage students to rebel."

"I'll hold you to that," he said. "See you around, Teach."

Before she could muster a reply, Chance Avery left the room. A grin stole across her face as she watched the door through which he had disappeared. And she hoped that, indeed, she would see him "around" very soon.

Chapter Two

Virile hunk, Chance thought with a grin that had failed to leave his face since he left the school. Incorrigible wasn't the word for her. Maddening was more like it. He pulled past the sign that read "Avery Kennels and Obedience School," marking the edge of his dog ranch. He couldn't believe he had stood in the classroom with a woman he had come to lambaste, and wound up having to deal with his own raging hormones!

He reached his house, a large ranch-style home that he had built fifteen years earlier, when he and his wife had opened the ranch. They had started with a one-bedroom matchbox cabin, but now, over the years, he had added enough rooms to make the house sometimes seem too big and empty. He didn't even want to think how empty it would be in a few years when Jeanie went off to college.

Spooner, his favorite German Shepherd, stirred from her resting place on the porch, stretched, and started down the steps to greet him. He stooped and scratched her chest. "How ya doin', girl?" He touched her pregnant stomach. "This is getting to be a heavy load, huh, girl? Don't worry. It won't be long now."

He started toward the door, but before he reached it, he heard the vibrating sound of music in the distance. The groomer in the kennels had turned the radio up too loud again. Chance had told him it made the dogs nervous, but the college veterinary student almost always did as he pleased when he thought Chance was away.

He went toward it, wondering what anyone would be doing in the building that hadn't been in use lately.

The moment he opened the door, ready to surprise his employee in the act of whatever misdeed he was up to today, he saw Jeanie standing on a platform, dancing without inhibition to the blaring music. She didn't see him as she jerked from side to side, holding an imaginary microphone.

Chance started toward the radio to turn down the music, when she began to sing out the lyrics of a popular song he had heard on the radio. Astounded, he stopped and listened to the quality of control in her voice, the zest in the belted words, the unique style in her delivery.

She was cute, bopping around up there like Tina Turner, he thought with a grin. And he had heard a lot of famous musicians who didn't sing this well. But admitting that to her, or himself, would lead to his admitting that she had any business at all belonging to a rock band. Which she did not. And he would tell her so today.

She made a half spin midchorus, and stopped suddenly when she saw him. "Daddy!"

Her face instantly blushed to a burning crimson, and she threw her hand over her mouth and scurried across the platform to turn off the tape player. "Why didn't you tell me you were here! It's sneaky to hide and watch someone without their knowing it!"

"I just got here," Chance said, grinning at the color scaling her cheeks. "You don't have to stop."

She looked up and flicked her waist-length blond hair back over her shoulder, and gave a half shrug, as if it hadn't mortified her to be caught acting like a fool. "I was just practicing for the gig Saturday night."

Chance's amusement faded instantly, and his own face paled at the same rate hers had blushed moments ago. "The what?"

"Gig, Daddy. It's what they call a show, a performance, a—"

"I *know* what a gig is," Chance said. "I just don't know what it has to do with you...especially this Saturday night."

Forgetting her embarrassment, Jeanie hopped down from the platform she had been standing on, her features alive as she came toward him. "It's a dance in the school gym, and they asked Scandal to play. It'll be my debut!"

"Scandal? That band is named Scandal?"

Jeanie giggled. "Daddy, chill out. It's just a name. I think it's a cool name for us."

"Jeanie, I told you, there is no 'us.' I haven't given you my permission to be in this band. It's one thing to sit around with friends and play a few instruments and sing, but there is no way in he—" He reminded himself that he was trying to stop cursing around his impressionable daughter. "No way in the world I'm going to let you do a 'gig' anywhere this Saturday night with a band named Scandal."

"But Daddy," she whined, flicking her hair back over her shoulder again and batting her green eyes at him—huge green eyes that never failed to melt his heart. "It's just a little high school dance. If I weren't playing, you'd let me go to it, anyway, wouldn't you?"

"Well, yes, but—"

"So what's the difference in my going to the dance to dance or going to the dance to sing?"

"There's a big difference," Chance said, knowing he wasn't standing on very sturdy ground. "You're too young to get up on a stage and perform like that."

"But that's not fair! If I follow all of your rules about dating and curfews, why is it wrong? Is it just because I'm enjoying myself? Is that against one of your rules?"

The unwavering tightness in Chance's face told her she'd gone too far, and she dipped her head and sighed as soon as she'd spat out the words. "That's enough, young lady," he said. "No matter how many times you've rehearsed this argument in your head, you can't bully me into letting you do this. I'm not ready for my daughter to be the central attraction at a high school dance!"

"But you weren't ready for me to start wearing makeup, either, Daddy. And you sure weren't ready to let me date. But *I* was ready."

Chance leaned back against a bare, dusty beam angling down from the roof to the floor and rubbed his face with his callused hands. Damn it, he thought, rehearsed or not, she was right. He had fought like a madman to stand in the way of her first date. The interrogations he had inflicted on the poor boy had been enough to put fear in an ax murderer. And he'd come up with excuse after excuse to keep her from learning to drive. When she'd broken down and accused him of not being fair, he had had to give in. If there was one button Jeanie knew how to push effectively, it was his sense of fair play.

The fact that she pushed that very button now didn't change his mind, however. It only forced him to rethink his strategy. This once, he would have to give in. But there wouldn't be a next time. "All right," he said, the words rolling out on a grudging sigh. "You can play under one condition."

A victorious smile cut across Jeanie's face. "Anything!"

"That I be a chaperon at the dance."

Jeanie's expression collapsed, and her eyebrows arched in distress. "Oh, Daddy, do you have to? That's so dorky."

"Don't worry," Chance said, his grin returning. "I'll do my best not to embarrass you. Then, after the dance, we're going to sit down and reevaluate this band situation again."

Jeanie tried the sad, sidelong gaze again, but Chance didn't let it sway him.

"Take it or leave it, kiddo."

Jeanie blew out a laborious breath. "All right," she said finally. "It's better than nothing, I guess."

Chance saw the spark returning to his not-so-little girl's eyes, and he had to smile sadly. "I'm not so sure about that," he said, starting toward the door.

Sometimes nothing was quite a bit better than something.

He opened the barn door, but turned back before leaving. "By the way, I met that teacher of yours today."

Jeanie's face twisted dramatically. "Simone? Oh, Daddy, you didn't!"

"Damn...darn right I did. I thought it was time we had a little talk."

"Terrific. I'll never be able to look her in the face again. Thanks a lot, Dad."

"Hey, your old man isn't that bad," he said with a grin. "I didn't do anything to embarrass you."

She gave him a dubious look. "Are you sure?"

"Positive," he said.

She looked at him for a moment, and a slow smile broke through her frown. "So what did you think of her? Isn't she cute?"

"That's not exactly the word I would have chosen," he said, as words like "bombshell," and "knockout" fleeted through his mind. "I'd say she was...interesting."

"She's a great teacher, too," she said. "All the kids love her."

He paused for a moment, neither inside nor outside the door. "So...is she married or what?"

Jeanie's knowing grin told him instantly that he never should have asked. "No, she's not married. Haven't I always called her 'Miss?'"

"Everybody calls their teachers 'miss.' Besides, you call her Simone most of the time, which really doesn't seem right for a teacher-student relationship...."

"She told us to call her that, Daddy. But why did you want to know if she was married?"

His grin was a little too revealing, and he said, "Just wondered if there was some poor soul I should feel sorry for. The woman would drive a sane man crazy in two weeks flat."

"Yeah, right," Jeanie said, not believing a word.

With a wry wink, Chance ambled out of the barn.

SIMONE KNEW THE MOMENT of truth had come when she pulled her van into her driveway and saw her brother Brian and his friend Joe-Joe, the bass player in Scandal, sitting on her front steps with wry grins on their faces. Bracing herself, she got out and started toward them. "Uh-oh. What's going on?"

"Your birthday," Brian said, raking his fingers through his tawny hair. "Your surprise is inside."

Simone studied the door, wondering if she, indeed, wanted to go through it. "So why aren't you in there with it?"

Their grins were the epitome of devilishness. "Because we wanted to stay out here and warn you."

"Warn me of what?"

Brian bit his bottom lip and tried to look innocent, but his effort produced the opposite effect. "Well, you know. At your age, we didn't want to give you too much of a surprise."

"At my age?" Simone repeated. "What am I gonna do? Have a heart attack?"

The boys snickered again, and knowing that she couldn't put it off any longer, Simone started for the door. "Brian, I hope you're keeping in mind that I'm a teacher and I have a reputation to uphold, and that

Edith Seal, the most busybody member of the school board, lives right across the street."

"Don't worry, Sis," Brian said on the edge of a laugh. "We won't tell anybody. And it would serve Mrs. Seal right if she did see your present. Maybe we should send him over to her, too."

"Him?"

The boys fell against each other guffawing, and Simone took a deep, fortifying breath and pushed open the door. A sharp, primitive drumbeat started instantly, followed by a sultry accompaniment on the stereo across her living room. Suddenly a man appeared from her hallway—a man dressed in a tight T-shirt, a hard hat and skintight jeans, much like the ones Chance Avery had worn today, she noted, jeans that threatened to burst open with every undulation of his rhythmic hips as he danced to the music and leered at her like a wild man after a month in solitary confinement.

Her first instinct was to scream out, stop the show and insist that the man go home before he took anything off. But that was just what her brother expected. What would he do, she wondered, if she called his bluff?

She went to the stereo, pretending she was going to cut off the music, but instead, she turned it up full-volume and flung around theatrically, grinning from ear to ear. Enjoying her reaction, the man began to pull his shirt over his head to the disturbing, if seductive, beat of the music.

"Take it off!" she shouted, then sent a loud whoop out over the music. Her brother and his friend stood just outside, chortling uncontrollably. She turned around and glared at Brian, wondering what he would do if she closed that door and disappeared into the house with the stranger. She ought to, just to show him, she thought. She should close that door and ask the stripper—the decidedly handsome stripper—to slip out the back way, thank you very much, *before* he had time to peel away any more of his clothes.

Instead she did nothing, and watched as the stripper began to release the button fly of his jeans . . . one by shocking one. But she didn't let herself appear shocked. Instead, she gave another loud, boisterous whoop, and cried, "Come on, baby! Come to Mama!"

Her brother and his friend literally screamed out their laughter, and she glanced toward the door to see them doubled over in painful hysteria.

It occurred to her that she should stop the whole thing right now, but it was too tempting to teach her brother a lesson. Besides, she had read that these guys never disrobed completely. As long as he followed the rules, she supposed she had nothing to fear.

He shed his pants, which left him in only a tight G-string that left little to the imagination. She fought the urge to pull the plug on the whole thing, and instead dug through her purse for a dollar bill.

The man grinned as she came toward him, waving it in the air. Not missing a beat, she folded the dollar bill and stuck it in his G-string.

The loud music was overpowered by Brian's and Joe-Joe's hysterical laughter, and finally Simone turned to the door, where her little brother rolled on the floor, clutching his stomach and wiping the tears from his face. "Brian, how long do I get him? Did you pay for a whole night?"

Before her brother could catch his breath to answer, she sensed someone else stepping into the open doorway. Quickly she glanced up and saw her neighbor, Edith Seal, gaping in horror.

Gasping, Simone spun around and dashed to the stereo to cut off the music, then grabbed the stripper's pants and thrust them into his arms.

"Hey, I'm not finished!" the dancer protested.

Simone turned back to the door, a sick feeling rising in her stomach. It was only then that Brian and Joe-Joe realized someone else was there.

"Mrs. Seal! How long have you been standing there?" Simone asked.

"Long enough! I came to ask you to turn the music down, but I had no idea there was an orgy going on over here!"

"An orgy?" She swung around to the stripper, who stood dumbly holding his pants. "I told you to get dressed!" she shouted.

Shrugging, he turned around, revealing the bare buns that the G-string did nothing to cover, and began stepping into his jeans.

"Mrs. Seal, this is hardly an orgy. My little brother was playing a practical joke on me for my birthday, and I was trying to give him a taste of his own medicine. Surely you don't think—"

"What I think is that this isn't the way a teacher in our school system should be conducting herself!"

Suddenly overwhelmed with the implications of Mrs. Seal's words, Simone decided to take the offensive. "Well, you wouldn't even *know* how I conduct myself if you hadn't been spying on me through my own front door. For your information, I was just about to send this...gentleman...on his merry way."

"Yes," the woman said, "and I suppose that's why you stuck money in his underpants and asked your brother if you could have him all night?"

"It was a joke, Mrs. Seal! You do remember what that is, don't you?"

"That man's naked body is no joke, Miss Stevens. And neither is your precarious position with this school system."

"Hey!" Brian came to his feet and turned on the woman. "My sister is the best teacher in that school. You can't blame her for something I did."

"Yeah," the stripper said, surprising Simone, as he began to button his fly. "Besides, I don't stay all night. I'm legit."

Suddenly the hilarity of the whole moment overcame her, and she had to bite back laughter. "Yeah, what kind of guy do you think he is?"

At once, she and Brian and Joe-Joe were all laughing together, and Mrs. Seal only gaped bitterly at them. "I see nothing amusing about this. But I can assure you, you haven't heard the last of it."

Simone's laughter died as she watched the woman storm off her porch, then turned back to the three men in her living room, unable to find the humor, herself, anymore. She glanced around the room, making a quick inventory, wondering how her brother could have used the key she had given him "in case of emergency" to let some stranger into her house to wander around alone. "Where's my dog?"

"I didn't see a dog," the hunk said grudgingly. "Just a small horse that kept trying to knock me down. I let him out back."

Without paying her birthday present further heed, Simone went to the kitchen and threw open the back door. Her dog, an Irish wolfhound that was every bit as big as she, though he had been tiny and cute just a few weeks earlier, bolted in, jumping up and setting his front paws on her chest, knocking her off balance. "Down, Dino!" she cried. "Down."

She groped for something to hold on to, found the back of a chair, and pulled herself aright. Then, trying to look dignified, though her hair was all tousled and her shirt was twisted, she turned back to her mischievous brother, his giggling friend and the half-dressed hunk pouting at her lack of appreciation.

"Thanks for the birthday present, Brian."

"Glad you liked it," he said. "I know Ol' Lady Seal did."

"You have no idea what she could do." She swallowed, and sighed. "It's nice to know that when I assured Jeanie Avery's father today that you were a nice, safe, stable kid he could trust his daughter with, I wasn't stretching the truth at all."

"Aw, come on, Sis," he said, laughing and handing the stripper a check. "It was just a joke. And hey, you got me. For a minute, I honestly thought you might jump his bones right there. I'm not convinced you wouldn't have if Mrs. Seal hadn't walked in."

Simone tried not to grin as he walked the disgruntled dancer to the door and, with a shrug, said, "Sorry."

"Yeah," the man said, slinging his shirt over his shoulder and starting out the door to the rusty pickup parked on the curb. "Can't gripe about easy money."

Simone glanced out the window and saw Mrs. Seal talking to a neighbor across the street. "Finish buttoning your fly before you go out there!" she shouted before he made it to the porch. The man turned back, and with a sexy grin that had a decidedly contagious edge, did as ordered.

Simone bit her lip to keep from smiling and leaned over to pet Dino.

She stole a look across the street, and saw Mrs. Seal and the neighbor gawking at the hunk again. This wasn't good, she thought, but there was no use worrying about it yet. The woman would use it against her when she least expected it, and there wasn't anything she could do to stop her.

Brian closed the door, and the huge dog promptly lifted his leg and relieved himself on her carpet. "See what you've done?" she accused. "You've gotten Dino all excited."

Flopping down on the couch, he regarded the spot on the rug. "We didn't do that. That dog lifts his leg every time someone smiles at him. What did Jeanie's dad say?"

"That he was making her get out of the band. He thinks Jeanie's too young." Deliberately she avoided mentioning that Chance considered Brian and his friends "walking hormones." That would only encourage their afternoon of irreverence, she thought.

"He can't," Joe-Joe said. "She's the best singer we've ever tried. She's the reason we've been getting all these gigs."

"All what gigs?" Simone asked, beginning to wonder if *any* of what she had told Chance today had been true.

"The school dance this Saturday night," Brian said. "At your school. And then in a couple of weeks, there's a ten-year class reunion over at the rec center."

"And a couple of big birthday parties after that—" Joe-Joe added. "She can't quit on us now. Can't you do something?"

Simone threw up her hands and went to the kitchen to get something to clean up Dino's mess. "Hey, I don't have anything to do with this. Her father thinks I'm some kind of idiot as it is, and when Mrs. Seal starts talking about that half-dressed centerfold who just left my house, my credibility is going to be a little thin."

She came back with a wet hand towel and some rug shampoo, and began scrubbing. "Dino, what am I gonna do with you?"

Brian popped up and started for the door. "Come on, Joe-Joe. We have to go talk to Jeanie." He threw Simone a glance over his shoulder. "Happy birthday, Sis. Sorry things got a little out of hand with your present."

"Next time buy me a cake."

"Mom bought you one," he said. "But she can't bring it tonight. She has a Tupperware party. And Dad already ate two pieces."

The door closed on her brother's laughter again, and Simone looked down at her canine friend. "Some birthday, huh?"

The dog just sprawled on his back, inviting her to pat his belly.

She slid down the wall at her back and rubbed her dog's hairy stomach. "Got beheaded at least three times today, tripped over that dress a hundred times, got chewed out by a man who thought I was some kind of flaky kid right out of college, got stripped for, got yelled at, got wet on..." She heaved a deep sigh and let her hand fall to the floor. Dino rolled to his feet. "And now it looks like I'm going to have to go to my parents' crazy house just to get a piece of my own birthday cake. Almost makes you want to skip the whole day, doesn't it?"

Dino licked her face and she pushed his head away. "Go gargle before you do that again, will you?"

She got up and started for the kitchen, wondering what she would cook for herself tonight, and why she hadn't agreed to go out with one of the three men who had offered to celebrate her birthday with her. Because there wasn't one among them who would add anything significant to the day she was born, she thought.

She thought of her brother's good intentions, and realized it was just his way of loosening her up. He'd told her too often lately that she needed to let herself get involved with someone again, but after the last time, she found it too difficult. There was too much risk involved in relationships, she told herself. Men weren't trustworthy creatures; they enjoyed breaking women's hearts. She wasn't one of those women who needed a man for completion, but it had been her experience that having a man often meant tearing herself apart. It just wasn't worth it.

Still, a fleeting thought passed through her mind, of Chance Avery, his hand on the side of her ribs, tugging at her zipper. He had gotten quiet—too quiet—when he'd watched her peel off that dress. And then he'd come out with the question about her age.

A grin tiptoed across her lips, and she thought that just maybe that was the best present she could have had on her thirtieth birthday, after all. A man who got her blood pumping and suggested she looked like a kid, on the very day when she felt her youth slipping away.

Yes, her assessment of men probably applied just as much to him as it did to any other man she'd encountered, but that didn't keep him from strutting through her mind, teasing with her feminine urges. Just because she had a clear picture of men didn't mean she disliked them completely. Some of them were hard to shake out of her mind.

For a fleeting moment, she allowed herself to consider what he might look like dancing to that primitive beat and undulating in a G-string. The thought made her face grow red, and she shook her head viciously and told herself she was letting this get way out of hand. She'd probably never even see him again. Unless, of course, he came to watch Jeanie sing when the band played for her school.

The possibility sent a soft smile skittering over her face, but she told herself he was simply a student's father, and the fact that he looked good enough to drool over was something she'd have to deal with. She would treat him like she treated any other man. With coolness and distance.

And if that proved ineffective, well, then, she'd just have to jump his bones. Throwing her head back, she laughed aloud, and admitted that turning thirty had destroyed a good number of brain cells. But what the heck, she thought, she had more than she needed, anyway!

Chapter Three

Glow-in-the-dark stars extolling the theme of "When You Wish upon a Star" twinkled above heads in the darkened high school gym, where a hundred students and their dates mingled, waiting for Scandal to begin playing. Chance smiled slightly as he stepped into the throng and looked toward the stage. It was still dark, though the band's equipment was set up, ready to go.

He glanced around at the teenagers dressed in outfits they'd probably shopped weeks for, looking for just the "right" thing, and marveled at how alike they looked. It never ceased to amaze him how contradictory kids were in wanting to stand out, yet blend in at the same time. He was glad Jeanie had more sense.

Again, his eyes gravitated toward the stage, and he wondered where his daughter was. She had left the house early in a pair of jeans, a sweatshirt and tennis shoes, saying that she'd change at the school since she'd probably get dirty helping to set up the equipment. She had been quieter than usual that day, spooky quiet, and it hadn't taken him long to realize that she was nervous about the performance. Singing on a crate in an empty barn was one thing, but singing in front of all of her peers was another. He shook his head and told himself that he wouldn't have had the nerve...not in a million years. He would have bet that Jeanie wouldn't, either, but in this one case he supposed her stubbornness might pay off. She was more determined than she was scared, he thought, and she had something to prove. To him, if no one else.

"So you finally got here."

Chance swung around and saw Simone Stevens grinning up at him. Had she been that little when he had seen her the other day? he asked himself. Had her eyes been that blue? And had she had that drop-dead figure that made his pulse accelerate?

Yes, he answered himself. The truth was that she had, and that was why he hadn't been able to get her out of his mind since.

"Were you waiting for me?" he asked.

She grinned and shot him a disarming look. "No, I wasn't waiting for you. But Jeanie told me you were coming. She was a little nervous about it."

"Jeanie was nervous, period. I doubt my coming had anything to do with that."

"She really wants you to approve," Simone added. "But she's excited. I've never seen so much sparkle in her eyes."

The sparkle in Simone's eyes seemed to intensify with the words, distracting Chance momentarily, and he let his gaze move to her hair, long and luscious and curly—the kind of curly that had nothing to do with frizz, the kind that he suspected was natural rather than permed. That gaze dropped to her blouse, red and silky, tucked into a pair of black slacks. Her clothes were conservative enough for his taste. And yet something about her subtle scent, or the way she stood in her high heels, or the way her eyes looked so directly into his...

Yes, he told himself, it had been way too long since he had been with a woman.

As if she recognized his scrutiny—and enjoyed it—Simone held out her hands and struck a pose. "So what do you think? Do I look more my age today? Do I look more like a teacher?"

"I don't know about looking like a teacher, but you sure don't look like a kid anymore."

Was it his imagination, or did her face redden just a little as she grinned up at him? He felt his own growing hot and wondered if the school was going to turn on the air conditioners tonight. His eyes trailed to the opening in her blouse, but he forced them back up to her face.

"I mean, no miniskirts or bare shoulders, and your hair's normal...not in some crazy hairdo like some of these."

"No, I gave up miniskirts when I quit ironing my hair and sold my go-go boots."

"Now that's something I would like to have seen," he said. "Although I have no objections against what I see right now."

She glanced down at his white dress shirt with tiny black stripes threading through, then down to the black trousers he had gotten from the cleaners that day. "You don't look so bad yourself," she said, as if he had paid her a blatant compliment.

A slight grin tugged at his lips, and he started to thank her, when a student grabbed Simone's arm. With a wink, she turned away from him, and he watched her being whisked into a giggling crowd of teenagers. A feeling of frustration swirled through him, like a dance partner who got cut in on, and he told himself he hadn't come here to see her, anyway. He had come to see Jeanie.

Chance strolled over to the punch table and poured himself a glass, then found a bare place against a wall and leaned back, watching Simone interacting with her students. She could win the most-popular-teacher award hands-down, he mused, but that didn't mean she was a *good* teacher. It only meant that she gave the kids what they wanted. Not necessarily what was best for them.

And it was also because she was such a knockout. She was every high school boy's fantasy, with that rich brown hair that looked so satiny to the touch and those full lips that always seemed to be smiling and those effervescent eyes.... And the body...the very thought of which made his groin tighten...

The drummer did a drumroll on the stage, snatching Chance's attention from Simone, and he pushed off from the wall and looked for Jeanie. A spotlight shone at center stage, and as the drummer continued playing, the crowd got quiet and all attention centered there.

He saw Simone break free of the crowd and start toward him, her face animated with excitement as she watched the stage.

The keyboard player dashed out like an international star and joined the drummer on his piano. Next came the bass player, and then Brian on guitar, and the group launched into a Paula Abdul tune as the students began coupling off and drifting onto the dance floor.

Then suddenly from offstage a girl's voice rose over the speakers and Jeanie burst onto the stage like Madonna coming to greet her fans. And as she entered the spotlight at center stage, Chance saw for the first time that night what his daughter was wearing. But it wasn't the ridiculous clothes—multicolored tights under a tiny leather miniskirt, a tight neon-orange shirt with a bare middle—that concerned him the most.

Chance's face paled and he gaped at his child. "Her hair's blue," he muttered. "Tell me that's the light. Tell me her hair isn't really blue."

Simone's laughter rose over the music. "Oh, it's blue all right. I helped her do it."

Chance turned on her, completely ignoring the song his daughter mastered on the stage. "You what?"

"Sure," Simone said without remorse. "I brought her the bottle. I thought it might give her a little self-confidence... to look so completely different."

"You told her to dye her hair *blue?*" he shouted over the noise.

For the first time, Simone noticed that he wasn't just yelling to be heard over the music. "Well... yes. But don't worry. It washes out."

"Her hair is *blue!*" he repeated. "How dare you tell my daughter to do something like that? Do you know what stuff like that leads to?"

"No, what?"

"It leads to... all sorts of things. Decadence, defiance... I don't want my daughter's hair blue!"

"Well, I told you it washes out! By the time she goes to bed tonight, her hair will be back like it was."

"Just because it washes out, you think it's okay? Tell me something, Teach. Who's going to wash it out of her new, 'improved' personality? Huh?"

Simone knew better than to laugh out loud, but she couldn't help the tiny grin sneaking across her lips. "If it stained personalities, Mr. Avery, I think it would have a warning on the label."

"Damn you!" he shouted.

The curse startled her, and her smile faded as he turned and shoved furiously through the swinging doors that led out into the corridor.

SIMONE WATCHED THOSE doors swing independently in his wake, and she realized that he wasn't just annoyed. He was mad. And maybe he had a right to be.

She glanced over her shoulder at the stage and saw that Jeanie seemed to have settled into her element, singing her heart out and playing like a pro to the dancing audience. Sighing, she pushed through the doors and looked up the empty corridor where Chance was pacing, raking his stiff fingers through his hair.

"Look, Mr. Avery, I'm really sorry. I obviously overstepped my bounds by suggesting the dye. I didn't know you'd react like this."

"Damn right you overstepped your bounds. You had no right."

"All right. I was wrong. I can admit that. But don't just write off the whole night because of it. She's doing great up there, and she really wanted you to hear her...."

"No daughter of mine is going to cavort on some stage with blue hair!" he railed. "I have a good mind to make her get off right now."

"Come off it!" Simone threw back. "It's not like she got a tattoo!"

Chance stopped his pacing midstride and looked at her with stricken eyes. "A tattoo? Is that something I should be preparing myself for? Some new fad?"

That grin broke back through her facade, and Simone laughed in spite of herself. "No. How old *are* you, anyway?"

Indignant, as though he recognized the implication that he was old and out of touch, he rallied with, "Hey, if that's another crack about my being a stuffed shirt, I'll have you know that I like rock and roll as much as anybody. *I* was at Woodstock! But this isn't just music. It becomes a whole way of life."

"If you were at Woodstock, then that explains your distorted view of these things. Just because you pranced around naked with a bunch of hippies freaked out on LSD, you think your daughter is going to do that, too."

"I did not prance around naked!" he shot back. "I don't know what you've heard, Teach, but Woodstock was a spiritual experience."

"One you'd never allow for your daughter, am I right?"

"Damn right." He stared at her for a long moment, and suddenly he broke into a grudging grin that started in his eyes.

"That's a double standard," she pointed out with the beginnings of a grin of her own.

"That's what parenthood is all about," he said. "Double standards. Do as I say, not as I do. Like I told you, I was once a teenager myself, and I remember it well. I want Jeanie to fare a little better out there than I did."

"You can't write the script for her, Mr. Avery. She's got to live it for herself."

His eyes were softer now, and Simone thought how it was worth his wrath just to get to that smile. Those lines around his eyes crinkled like half rainbows, making that smile seem even more natural than she would have imagined.

"Chance," he said. "Don't call me Mr. Avery. It only reinforces that too-old-to-know-what's-going-on image that I hate."

"All right," she said. "But you have to call me Simone. Nobody calls me Miss Stevens unless they're mad at me."

When he didn't argue that, for consistency's sake, he had better stick with Miss Stevens, she smiled and reached for his hand. "You know, Chance, I don't think it's the music or the clothes or the blue hair that's got you worried. I think if that shirt of yours *is* stuffed, it's just possibly stuffed with a reformed renegade. Maybe you're afraid Jeanie has more of you in her than you want."

"You may be right," he confessed. "I've sowed a wild oat or two in my day. And just because I've cleaned up my act, it doesn't mean that I'm a stuffed shirt. I'm starting to think I might have to take drastic action to convince you of that."

Her grin was a little too sexy for her own good. "The possibilities are intriguing," she said, "but how about if I just take your word for it?"

"Oh, I can't leave it at that," he said. "No, I'm going to have to set you straight somehow."

Her heartbeat sped up with the tempo of the music, and she held his gaze for a long moment, wondering if she should do as she had done with Brian and call his bluff... or turn and run like hell.

But she had never been much for running, so instead she decided to douse the moment with a bit of reality. "You could always dye your hair blue," she said with a grin.

As it was intended, the comment snapped his attention back to his chagrin over his daughter, and his expression quickly collapsed. "One blue-hair in the family is enough, thank you very much." He went to the door, peered through the glass at his daughter singing on the stage.

Simone came up beside him. "Look at her, Chance," she said softly. "She's blossoming. Everybody's dancing, which means they like her, and she looks like she's been performing for years. And *listen* to her. She's fantastic."

Looking through the glass, Chance had to admit that his daughter's shyness seemed to have fled away like the true color of her hair. "She is good, isn't she?"

"Too good," she said. "You can't stop her now, Chance. She's had a taste of it. Let her stay in the band. Give her the benefit of the doubt. If you've raised her as well as I think you have, you don't have to worry."

Chance didn't commit, but he didn't discard the idea completely. And when Simone pushed open the door and pulled him back into the gym behind her, where Jeanie's voice filled the room in all its talent and glory, Chance had to admit that this time Simone might just be right.

THE LIGHTS ON THE STAGE were hot and bright, but on the outer perimeters of the dance floor Jeanie saw her father standing with Simone, watching her dance to the bridge of the song as Brian embarked on his guitar solo.

Her father's smile lightened her heart and she told herself that was a good sign. Maybe her singing had distracted him from her hair color, she thought. Either that or Simone had.

The solo ended and Jeanie launched into the Gloria Estefan song that had the whole dance floor packed. If she had been down there among her peers, she probably wouldn't have even had a date. And now, here she was, the star of the show.

And she liked that stardom even more than she had expected.

Her eyes danced as she skipped across the stage, belting out the lyrics, and she met Brian's gaze. Picking up on her flirtatious dance, he sidled up to her and slid his fingers across the strings, grinning at her. And as she sang and moved back and forth to the upbeat rhythm, Brian picked up the same step, so that the two looked as if they had been choreographed.

Laughing, he fell back as she belted out the last of the song, and when the drummer ended it with a short drumroll, Jeanie swung around, seeking his approval.

"That was great," Brian said. "Keep it up. They love you."

The words filled her right where she needed to be filled, and tearing her eyes from the pastel blueness of his, she listened for the intro to the next song, a slow one.

Her eyes collided with her father's and she saw that he was flashing her a thumbs-up, and her heart soared. And then she saw Simone reach for his hand and coax him onto the dance floor.

Not for the first time, it occurred to her what a cute couple the two of them would make, and as her father reluctantly pulled Simone against him and began to dance, an idea occurred to her.

"I'd like to dedicate this next song to my two favorite people in the world," she said into the mike. "My father and my teacher. Chance Avery and Simone Stevens."

The students applauded, and Jeanie broke into the sexy Mariah Carey song, "Vision of Love," as her mind began concocting schemes to reach the goal she had so suddenly set for herself.

CHANCE DIDN'T TRY to hide the look of dread on his face at the dedication, but Simone didn't seem daunted.

"Don't look so miserable," Simone teased. "My students will think I stepped on your feet. They're watching us, you know."

He looked down at her, and found it difficult to resist the smile that always seemed to dwell in her eyes. "I can't believe she did that."

"She did, though. Now smile and pretend you're dancing with me because I'm irresistible."

His grin broke through and he breathed a laugh that swept across her lips. Her heart stumbled and she stepped on his foot. "Sorry."

"It's okay," he said. "You walk on the top and I'll walk on the bottom."

She laughed. "I'll walk on my own, thank you. I used to be a pretty darn good dancer, but it's been a while."

"Uh-huh," he said doubtfully.

She smiled up at him. "And what is that supposed to mean?"

His grin looked even more sexy up close, and she wondered how soft his laugh lines would be to the touch. "It means that I can't see you spending too many nights sitting at home."

"I'll have you know that I spent my *birthday* sitting at home."

He frowned around his grin. "You're kidding. Why?"

She shrugged and let her eyes gaze off over his shoulder. "Didn't have anything better to do than eat popcorn with Dino."

"Dino?"

"My dinosaur...or my dog. I haven't yet decided what he is, but I do know he's hairy and is shaped like an Irish wolfhound, although he's growing at the rate of a stegosaurus. It could go either way."

Chance began laughing again, for no good reason, and he marveled at how good it felt. "So you sat home with Dino and ate popcorn on your birthday, huh? My heart is bleeding for you."

"It should," she teased. "Especially after you lambasted me that afternoon. I almost never got over it. Even the stripper didn't help."

"The what?"

She laughed then, realizing she'd almost said too much, and shook her head. "Never mind. It was the practical joke I'd been expecting."

She dropped her face to his shoulder, cutting off the conversation, and Chance pulled her closer without meaning to. He glanced up at his daughter, who had her eyes closed and was singing with all her soul. The soft, sweet scent of some perfume he couldn't name wafted up from Simone's hair, and he grinned at her description of her dog again. And the stripper? He could only imagine.

The song got close to the end, and he felt himself dreading letting Simone go. It felt too good holding her this close, without commitment, without it even being his idea, but he wasn't naive enough to expect the band to play two slow numbers back-to-back. Not at a high school dance where the kids would rather sweat-dance than pet-dance. The petting went on outside, out of the sight of the chaperons.

Of course, when the chaperons were preoccupied, as he had been for the past half hour...

The song ended and he let her go and told himself he wouldn't dance with her again. He hadn't come here to spark romance like one of the teenagers, he told himself. He had come here to keep an eye on his daughter.

It wasn't his fault if that eye kept straying to the little teacher whose scent promised to keep him awake all night.

He looked down at her as she laughed up at him and thanked him for the dance, and wondered what it would hurt to ask her out to dinner. Then quickly he told himself that it would be foolhardy. Chance had enough problems without being attracted to a woman who had already caused trouble in his life.

He looked once again at his daughter, who was rubbing shoulders with Brian and flirting with the drummer as she sang, and told himself that Simone was wrong about her brother not being a walking hormone. Chance would have known that look anywhere. And damn it, he didn't like it being directed at his daughter.

Stiffening, he went to the wall and leaned back as Simone joined him. "You still aren't comfortable with this, are you?"

Chance shook his head. "Would you be, if your daughter was alone so much with four boys at the peak of their sexuality, dancing and flirting and singing..."

"Brian's a nice boy," Simone said again.

"Nice boys have fantasies, too," he said, meeting her eyes.

"Do they?" she asked with a half grin.

He couldn't help matching that grin, and his eyes dropped ever so quickly to the shape of her breasts beneath the silky red blouse. Suddenly he wished she weren't quite so appropriately dressed. He would have loved to see her blouse unbuttoned just a little more, and the hint of the swell of her breasts peaking out just a little. "Yes, they do," he said, knowing his voice was growing husky. "And some of them don't control them that well."

"Is that so?" she asked, her voice dropping to a husky pitch.

"Mmm-hmm," he said. "What about nice girls? Do they have fantasies?"

"Some do," she said with a grin that made his mouth go dry. "But they know better than to feed them."

"What if someone else feeds them?" he asked. "What then?"

She dropped her lids the slightest degree and peered up at him. "What have you got in mind?"

The question almost startled him, but he couldn't let it die. His grin slipped further across his face. "What makes you think I'm talking about me?"

"I don't think you'd have that look in your eye if you were talking about Jeanie," she whispered. "And all this talk about fantasies..."

"I was talking about so-called 'nice boys,'" he said. "No one ever said that description fit me."

Simone's grin almost drove him insane as she looked up at him, sizing him up for just what he did mean. And as she seemed to look right through him, to the origins of all the innuendos and implications, he wondered if she would see that he really didn't even know himself. All he knew was that he hadn't been this attracted to a woman in years, and there was nothing he would like more than to do something about it.

But playing out fantasies almost always led to emotional entanglements, and those were just too complicated. He had enough problems right now, with a teenage daughter busting out all over and a business to run. The last thing he needed was to get involved with someone who just might drive him completely crazy.

But risk wasn't something Chance Avery was used to running from, especially when his own hormones were involved. And he knew that curiosity about her would keep him awake nights until he had had one taste of the promise smoldering in her eyes.

Chapter Four

The last song ended promptly at midnight, but the students didn't rush to get home. Many lingered behind in the gymnasium, exchanging last-minute goodbyes before their parents picked them up outside or negotiating for rides home with friends and potential dates.

Feeling like the Queen on Coronation Day, Jeanie turned to Brian, who was unplugging his guitar and setting it back in its case. "Well? Did we do okay?"

Brian's smile was genuine, if preoccupied. "We did great. You slew them, Jeanie. They loved you."

She stooped down next to the case and looked up at him with hopeful eyes. "I don't know how I'll get home," she said, knowing the hint was too obvious but not knowing a better way to ask. "I rode here with Cathy, my friend. She was on the dance committee, but she's about to leave."

Brian glanced in the direction of the girl they spoke of. "Well, if you need to, you can go on home with her." He glanced toward Simone and Chance, and a wicked grin eased across his face. "Or you could team up with destiny and give your dad a good excuse to ride home with my sister."

Jeanie glanced at her father, who seemed to be deeply engrossed in conversation with Simone. She had never seen his eyes smile like that when he talked to a woman, and she wondered if she were just now old enough to notice something like that. Or was it simply that he was as intrigued with Simone as she had hoped he would be? "That's an idea," she told Brian, realizing he wasn't going to take her bait and offer her a ride home. "They do seem to like each other, don't they?"

"Seem to," Brian said, wrapping the guitar cord around his arm. "And you have to know Simone like I know her, to realize how significant that is. She's the proverbial man-hater."

"Simone? Why?"

"She's been dumped on a lot," he said matter-of-factly. "Almost got married once. She hasn't sworn off men entirely, but she tells herself she can do without them."

"Well, my dad's not any average man," Jeanie said. "He might just be what she needs."

"Hey, no argument from me," Brian said. "I say you tell 'em how bad you need the car, and leave the rest to them." He held up a hand for a high-five, and slapping it, Jeanie stepped off the stage, ready to set her father's romance in motion.

CHANCE SAW JEANIE coming toward him, and instantly wiped that flirtatious look off his face and tried to look more appropriately parental. He couldn't help noticing the musicians watching her as she walked, and he wanted to drag them to the back room and tell them to keep their eyes and hands off his daughter if they placed any value on their lives at all.

"Hi, Daddy."

Simone nudged him with her elbow, indicating that he should heap her with praise over her performance. "Hi, sweetheart. You did great tonight. Everybody loved you." *Especially those sex-crazed man-shaped hormones on the stage.*

"Well...I have a little problem. Cathy's going home now, and I need to stay and help them break down the equipment. It's part of being in the band, Daddy, and I don't want special favors just because I'm a girl. But I won't have a ride home, unless I ride with one of the band members..."

Chance's first thought was disappointment that he wouldn't be able to pursue his fantasy of being alone with Simone, a fantasy he had to admit she had fed in her own way tonight. His second thought was that he felt guilty for putting his own needs before his child's. "I can wait for you and take you home," he said.

"No!" she whispered harshly. "That would be too embarrassing. I can't have my daddy waiting to take me home. Besides, I don't know how long it'll take. I've never done this before."

"Then what have you got in mind?" Chance asked. "Am I supposed to hitchhike home?"

"Well, I thought...maybe Simone could take you?"

His eyes darted to Simone's, and he wondered if it was consternation or alarm he saw there.

"That'll be fine," she said, surprising him and meeting his eyes directly. "I'll be glad to give you a ride home."

"Great!"

The enthusiasm in Jeanie's voice, not to mention her eyes, shook him, and he told himself this wasn't going the way he'd wanted. Yes, he'd wanted the chance to be alone with Simone, but he hadn't planned to let his daughter know the first thing about it. It wasn't healthy, having her get her hopes up about an attraction that was probably only physical.

"I don't know," he said, turning back to his daughter. "I don't see why I can't just wait around here for you to get finished...."

"Come on, Chance," Simone interrupted. "Let the girl go work. I'll get you home safely. I rarely have accidents, and when I do my passengers almost always come out in one piece."

Chance's attention was momentarily diverted from his daughter to the grinning teacher. "Almost always?"

"Yes," she said. "There was that nasty little incident a few years ago where my car flipped and my brother fell out the window and down a hill, but that was only because the road was slippery...."

"What?"

Simone laughed out loud. "I'm kidding. I've never had a wreck in my life, and as you can see, my brother is alive and well...."

Chance met her grinning eyes, and realized that, perhaps, she really did want the opportunity to be alone with him, as well. It was a gift he couldn't walk away from, and physical or not, the attraction was there.

"All right, Jeanie," he said, digging the car keys out of his pocket and handing them to her. "Don't be too late. And please don't go to bed with your hair like that. I hate to think what that dye will do to the pillowcases."

Jeanie stifled a grin and nodded. "I won't, Daddy. And thanks."

She turned and half ran, half pranced, back up the steps to the stage, and Chance watched her, feeling uneasy about leaving her here with those sweating musicians.

Simone took Chance's arm and began pulling him toward the door. "Come on, Pop. She'll be fine."

"Damn, I hate that blue hair," he said.

Simone couldn't help giggling as she dragged him away.

THE AIR WAS CRISP and smelled of impending rain and that subtle Simone scent that had tantalized Chance all night. Car engines revved and roared as students said their goodbyes through rolled-down windows, and the sound of laughter lilted over the breeze.

Across the parking lot, a group of kids saw their teacher with Chance, and shouted, "Good night, Simone. Don't do anything *we* wouldn't do."

Simone laughed and waved as she climbed into her minivan. Feeling self-conscious, Chance got into the passenger seat. "Do they all call you Simone?"

"Um-hmm," she said, navigating her way through the idling cars and loitering teens.

"Do you think that's a good idea?" he asked. "I mean, wouldn't they respect you more if they had to treat you like any other teacher?"

"I'm not any other teacher," she said. "And they do respect me."

"But a teacher isn't supposed to play the role of friend any more than a parent is," he said. "If you're their buddy, you lose your effectiveness as an authority figure."

"Authority isn't all it's cracked up to be," she said. "I'm not in this for some big power trip, and my students appreciate that. You can enjoy a kid a lot more if you aren't constantly trying to change him."

"Yeah, well, tell that to a father whose daughter has just come home pregnant by some nomad biker."

Simone grinned at the exaggerated picture and glanced at Chance. He was staring out the window, jaw propped on his hand. "You're brooding about leaving her there," she said. "Not that I'm criticizing, mind you. Brooding does look good on you. It's just that I prefer seeing those laugh lines in their natural state."

A grin began to work at the corners of his mouth. "And what state is that?"

"You know," she said, smiling across the van. "All crinkled up."

He laughed aloud, and her smile softened as she noted the sparkle in his eyes and the white perfection of his teeth. The question suddenly crossed her mind, tugging at her consciousness.

Why hasn't some woman snapped him up?

Maybe he hadn't made himself available, she told herself. Maybe he was too wrapped up with Jeanie to ever make concessions involving himself.

She glanced at him again, and saw that his smile had fallen back into that brooding state that made him so complex and intriguing. He was genuinely concerned about his daughter, and for some reason that seemed alien to her, that touched her deeply.

"You know, Jeanie has to grow up sometime," she said softly.

"I always expected her to, *sometime,*" he returned. "I just didn't expect it to be so soon...or in just this way."

"She's still a kid," Simone consoled. "She's just found a new way of expressing herself. I'm glad you let her perform tonight. It meant a lot to her that you saw her and approved."

"Approved?" Chance asked, looking over at her across the darkness. "Did I say I approved?"

"Well, you certainly calmed down after you got used to the hair. I mean, you didn't have to go pace the hall anymore after that, and I only saw your fists clench and your nostrils flare a couple dozen more times."

He laughed then and shifted in his seat to look at her, and she felt that familiar heat creeping back up her cheekbones. "You know, I do appreciate your giving me a ride home."

"No problem," she said, her smile fading slightly. "I know it wasn't exactly what you wanted to do, but..."

He could see that she was fishing and he liked it. Apprehension looked nice on her. "The truth, Teach, is that I was trying to decide whether to ask you out or not, anyway. Jeanie just made it all a little easier."

Simone's grin returned, and she glanced across the van at him. "What was the big decision? You either ask or you don't."

"I'm real bad with rejection," he said. "I wasn't sure you'd say yes. After all that talk about hormones and fantasies...I was afraid I might have scared you off." He paused and watched her smile fade again, and his heartbeat went into triple time. "I'm really not the aggressive type," he said. "I didn't want you to think there was anything to fear from me."

She swallowed and told herself that fear wasn't exactly the emotion she would have named. Excitement, perhaps. Exhilaration, maybe. Anticipation, certainly. "I'm not afraid of you," she said, wishing her voice didn't sound quite so shredded.

"Then how about if we don't go straight home?" he asked. "How about if we stop somewhere, have a drink, talk?"

"All right," she said. "Where?"

For a moment there was silence, and she glanced over at him.

He chuckled and gave a shrug. "I really don't have a clue. I don't do this very often."

"Go have a drink, or ask a woman to go with you?"

"Either," he said. "Where do you usually go?"

"I told you," she said, laughing, "I stay at home a lot with my dog, Dino. I happen to have a bottle of wine in the refrigerator. It's cheap and probably not very good, but I like it. If you want to go there for a little while..."

"Let's go," he said, and those laugh lines crinkled. "I'm looking forward to meeting Dino, and there's nothing I like better than cheap wine."

Simone smiled and turned the van around, heading for home.

SIMONE HAD BARELY opened the door when Dino lunged forward and, putting all his weight into his front paws as they reached her chest, knocked her down.

"Down, Dino! Stop it!" she cried, but Dino only straddled her and began licking her face. "Dino!"

She managed to squeeze out from under him and, shaken, came to her feet. "One of these days he's gonna knock me down and not let me up."

"Sooner than you think," Chance said, bending over to pet the animal that panted and sniffed at him. Lifting his leg, the dog issued a stream onto the carpet near Chance's feet. "Look what he did! This dog is too big to behave that way."

Throwing up her hands, she rushed into the kitchen for a towel, then hurried back to wipe up the mess. "Tell me about it," she said, falling to her knees. She began to rub up the wet spot, but Dino grabbed an end of the towel and began a tug-of-war. Giving up and letting go of the towel, she came to her feet, breathless. "But what am I supposed to do? You think teenagers are bad—"

"There's something you can do about dogs that you can't do for teens," Chance said, tackling Dino and forcing him to surrender the towel. Then kneeling, he began to scratch Dino's chest and the dog promptly rolled over. "It's called obedience training. I teach it at my kennels."

"Obedience training," Simone scoffed. "I don't like the sound of that."

"Really, Simone, it works. You'd be surprised. If I had a few sessions with Dino, I could change him.

He'd be a new dog. You wouldn't even recognize him."

"That's the problem. I like Dino. He's my best friend. So his spirit gets a little out-of-control at times. I don't want to break it by putting him through some militaristic training for dogs."

"So you'd rather *he* broke *you*? He's as big as you are, and he'll get bigger."

"Really?" Simone asked, wincing. "How much bigger?"

"It's hard to say," he told her, studying the dog's paws. "Irish wolfhounds can get huge. His paws are still pretty big, so his growth could be substantial over the next few months, depending on what you feed him."

"Hear that, Dino?" Simone asked, leaning over to scratch the panting dog's ear. "Guess that means no more hamburgers for you."

"Oh, my God. You don't feed the dog hamburgers?"

"I feed the dog whatever happens to be available. He supplements it by eating small children who happen to wander by my yard during the day."

Chance grinned and got to his feet, and as their smiling eyes locked together, she felt awkward, shy, like a teenage girl who didn't know how to act on a first date. "The wine's in . . . in the refrigerator."

"Which would be in the kitchen," he said.

She smiled and started out of the room. "I'll get us some glasses."

"I'll help," he said.

He followed her into the kitchen and leaned against the counter, and she realized her hands were shaking under his scrutiny as she struggled to pull the cork out of the bottle. She was nervous and it was so stupid. It wasn't like she was some kid who had never been with a man before!

"Here, let me," he said, and he took the bottle from her and pulled the cork out. He poured it into each glass, then recorked the bottle.

They each took a glass and quietly sipped, as their eyes locked together. The moment was maddening, and Simone asked herself why she couldn't banter with him now, as she had done on the dance floor. Why had she gotten as coiled up as a knot, just because they were alone?

As if he read her thoughts, he set down the glass, took her hand and pulled her closer.

"I've been wanting to do this all night," he whispered, and before she could react or understand or run, his lips were descending to hers.

The gentleness of his kiss swept through her like a warm ocean tide, and she curled into him and rose up on her toes and allowed herself to flow into the goodness and rightness of it. His wet lips opened over hers to deepen the kiss, and suddenly it wasn't enough, for there was so much more she wanted to explore in him.

Her arms slid up around his neck and she felt him tightening his embrace of her. Their bodies pressed together, and she felt his heart hammering against her breast.

His hair was silky to her touch, and she threaded her fingers through and told herself that it was too much at once. The taste, the touch, the scent, the security of him... It all had the potential to be addictive.

She broke the kiss and pulled back, but he didn't entirely release her from his embrace. She looked up at him, her eyes misty and smoky and confused.

"I'm not sure..." she began, but her voice sounded too breathless, too husky. She took a deep breath and tried again. "I'm not sure where you think this is going to lead."

"Where do you want it to lead?" he asked.

She shook her head. "I don't know...I mean, nowhere. Not tonight."

"No," he agreed. "Not tonight." He touched her face, pushed her hair back and let it thread through his fingers until the ends curled through them. "I'm not trying to get you into bed, Simone," he whispered. "But a little heavy petting never hurt anyone."

"Tell that to your daughter and see if you believe it," she said with a grin.

He dropped his hands to his sides and looked up at the ceiling, as if he realized she was right. The sudden release made Simone feel cold, lonely, and she fought the urge to pull those arms back around her and kiss him again.

"You're right," he said, bringing his eyes back to her again. "I shouldn't have kissed you."

"No," she protested. "You should have. I wanted you to."

"You did? Why?"

The question disturbed her, for she couldn't tell him why. *Because I've been panting over you since I mistook you for my little brother's birthday present.* She couldn't let him know that. "I just...did, that's all."

He took her hand and pulled her into the living room and sat down on the couch. Then he turned her to face him and pulled her onto the couch, half lying, half sitting, and propped her up with one strong arm.

"This is a little...close...isn't it?" she asked. "I mean if we're not going to do any heavy petting."

"Who said we're not?" he asked with a slow grin. "I happen to have every intention of heavy petting with you."

She gave him a surprised smile and tried to ignore the flutter of anticipation coursing through her. "I thought the comment about Jeanie had changed your mind."

"It might have for a minute," he admitted, "but that was before you told me you had wanted me to kiss you...and before I reminded myself that I'm a thirty-five-year-old man, and not a sixteen-year-old kid."

"Mmm," she whispered. "Sounds like you have this all figured out."

To prove her point, he pulled her closer and kissed her with more intensity and strength than they had kissed in the kitchen. And suddenly she felt like a sixteen-year-old kid herself, being swept away and completely out of control.

His lips dropped to her chin, then to her throat, and she felt his tongue stroking her chest at the V of her blouse. She shivered and arched her head back and he caught her neck again, nuzzled up to her ear, stroked the shell of it with his tongue....

She wondered how much she would regret it tomorrow if she unbuttoned her blouse just a little, if she moved his hand inside it, if she felt his skin against her flesh....

She heard a loud panting in her ear and something wet swept across her face. Startled, she looked up to see Dino trying to get into the act. He had propped his feet on the couch behind her, and began to whine for the attention that had so surprisingly been turned from him.

"Down, Dino," she said, trying not to spoil the mood. "Not now."

As if the dog had been called, he pulled his back legs up on the couch and licked Chance's face.

"Down, Dino!" Chance grabbed the dog's collar and tried to push him down, but Dino only became more determined to get some of the affection he had seen them sharing.

He drooled on Chance's arm and licked Simone's face again, and she grimaced and got up. "Dino, get down, now!"

"He's not going to respond to that voice!" Chance said, the beginnings of anger creeping into his face. "You have to be firm."

"Well, he's not listening to you, either!" she said.

"That's because you've spoiled him. He thinks he can do anything he wants." He stood up and jerked Dino's leather collar and forced him down. "Stay!" he ordered, and the dog looked up at him with sad eyes.

Chance turned to Simone. "Now, where were we?" he asked. But he saw from her eyes that the moment was shattered. The mood was destroyed.

She straightened her shirt, slipped her fingers through her hair and said, "Probably heading somewhere we shouldn't."

"You think?"

"I think."

He gave Dino a disgusted look. "Damn dog. Maybe he knew what he was doing, after all."

"Maybe."

He flopped back down on the couch and she sat a few feet away from him. The misery in both their faces was obvious. "You know, he really is too big to have that much freedom. Why don't you let me sign you up for my next obedience course? Really, it'll do you a world of good."

Simone straightened and looked him fully in the eye. "No thanks. It's Dino's good I'm concerned about. I'll just take my chances with him the way he is."

"But that's just asking for trouble," Chance pressed. "Don't you understand that if you don't nip this in the bud, your house is going to turn into the kind of free-for-all that you call a classroom?"

The comment smarted as soon as it hit her, and she sat up straight and lifted her chin. "I told you, my classroom is not a free-for-all. My students have learned more about history in my class than they've learned their entire lives."

"Well, we aren't talking about your students. They have parents to control them. We're talking about this barking, urinating, slurping hippopotamus just begging to be disciplined."

She tightened her lips and tried to suppress her rising anger. "All right, Chance. Why don't you tell me what kind of discipline you mean? Beating him? Caging him? Depriving him of food?"

"Of course not," he said. "A lot of it has to do with your tone of voice and the way you hold his choke collar—"

"By choking him? Is that how you do it?"

"You're missing the whole point. When the course is finished, the dog is happier because he knows his boundaries. Everybody around him is happier, because they aren't constantly being challenged and threatened."

"I see," she said, her tone becoming clipped. "You want to take my wonderful, happy, high-spirited dog and make a docile, frightened, shivering puppy out of him."

"Simone, that isn't—"

"Tell me, Chance," she said, "do you apply your dog-training methods to your daughter, as well? If so, maybe that's why she has such a problem with self-esteem."

Now she could see that the anger in Chance's eyes matched the burgeoning anger in her own. "If you think I should let my daughter run wild, so I won't 'break' her spirit, then you and I are even farther apart than I thought."

"I don't condone running wild," she said. "But I don't believe in cages, either."

She got up and grabbed her purse, dug out her keys and gestured for the door. "Now, if you're finished insulting my dog, *Mr.* Avery, I'll drive you home. I'm getting tired of this conversation."

"The feeling is mutual," he returned, knowing it was the most childish thing he could say. But somehow he couldn't help himself. Simone seemed to have a way of pulling the boy out of the man, and taking him through the gamut of his emotions, from fury to fever, from passion to anger. The longer he stayed, the more of a roller-coaster ride he would encounter.

And just when they got to the good parts, that damn dog would intervene.

Not arguing, he followed her out the door.

AS SIMONE SCREECHED OFF, leaving Chance standing in the night alone, he decided that he hadn't exactly given her an easy time of it tonight, either. After riding home in complete silence, he had made her let him out at the gate of his property, for it seemed too intimate to invite her all the way up the driveway. He slammed out of her van, hoping she got the message. He didn't like being treated like a tyrant.

But then she had done her little wheelie and taken off into the night, leaving him to feel that she had gotten the "last word" after all. Damn it, he thought. Why did he let that woman get to him so? And why was he so disappointed, and so tremendously let down, and so fantastically frustrated that their intimacy had ended before it had had a chance to begin?

He trekked up the dirt driveway and went into the dark, empty house. Jeanie must not have made it home yet, he thought, and he fought the panic rising inside him and told himself that she was fine. She'd probably be home soon.

He dropped into his recliner, turned on the lamp and stared at the blank television screen across the room. But he couldn't shake the memory of the way he had felt when he was holding Simone, kissing her, tasting her neck and her chest and wondering what she would do if he unbuttoned her blouse...

He had no business worrying about his daughter's behavior, when his was even more adolescent than hers, he thought. Necking with her teacher...it was more ridiculous than he would have believed. And yet his heart hadn't had such a workout in months, and he didn't remember ever wanting a woman quite so much.

He closed his eyes and tried to put thoughts of Simone out of his mind, but his body wouldn't forget. It would take some concentration, some denial and a lot of self-control to keep from calling her. But somehow he would have to get through it.

JEANIE FOUND HER FATHER still up when she got home. Quietly she came into the living room, knowing he hadn't heard her drive up, and saw him staring at the blank screen.

She had seen him do it many times; it was how he got lost in his thoughts. Sometimes she wondered if he saw his thoughts played out on that television screen, or if he even knew he was doing it.

"Hi, Daddy," she said softly, not wanting to disturb the quiet.

He looked up, startled, and winced at the sight of her hair again. "I didn't hear you come home."

"Did you have fun with Simone?" she asked.

He frowned. "Not particularly. She brought me home. End of song. Lord, I hate your hair that color."

"I'll wash it out in a minute, Daddy," she said, coming to sit on the arm of his chair. "But tell me what you thought."

A slow grin eased across his face and he knew she was fishing for a compliment. "About what?"

"About me. About the band. Were we fantastic or what?"

Chance pretended to consider the question, then grinned and gave her what he knew she wanted. The truth. "You were fantastic," he said grudgingly, losing his smile with the effort. "I wasn't crazy about the outfit or the hair, and I don't much like my little girl being the center of attention, bopping around and shaking her hips—"

"Oh, Daddy," she said, rolling her eyes. "What about the singing? Did you like how I sang?"

"You were terrific," he said, his eyes softening. "Just like your mother. It constantly amazes me how much you're like her. . . ."

His voice caught and trailed off, and Jeanie diverted her eyes to the screen, as if she, too, could see his thoughts there. He always got quiet when he spoke of her mother, as if she were some saint who deserved some degree of reverence. That he loved her was never a question, but Jeanie had been around her mother's sisters and mother enough to know that Amanda had had a tiny little wild streak before she had settled down and had a family. The stories they told of her in regular, sometimes irreverent, voices, had always made her laugh.

The only sadness she felt in relation to her mother was that she had never really known her. There were times when she wished for a mother's advice, or a mother's gentleness, or a mother to balance the rigidity her father sometimes displayed. But mostly, when she thought of her mother, it was with a warm, sweet feeling planted back in her toddler years, and a smile at the stories of her wild days.

She wondered what her mother would have thought of her singing tonight.

"Then you're going to let me stay in the band?" she ventured.

Chance looked up at her. Jeanie had no doubt in her mind that he wanted to say no. If his sense of fair play allowed it, he would demand that she turn in her microphone and wear her hair in pigtails again. But she also knew him well enough to know that he knew better.

"You know, this is hard for me," he said, reaching out to touch his little girl's blue hair. "Real hard. Harder than you'll ever know."

He dropped his hand and studied her seriously. "I know that sometimes it seems that I'm overprotective, Jeanie, and that I'm unreasonable. I know that sometimes I hover over you, and that it isn't easy for me to let go."

Her eyes were wide as she listened, waiting for the punch line.

"It's just that you're all I've got, and I love you. And sometimes it may just be that I'm overprotective for selfish reasons. I really hate to see you grow up. I hate to have to trust the people around you. I hate to lose control."

"I know you do, Daddy," she said, keeping her voice calm and steady, for she knew that his emotions would be easily tilted either way right now.

"But the truth is, I can't really come up with a logical enough reason to tell you to stay out of the band."

Jeanie squealed and lunged forward, throwing her arms around him. "Thank you, Daddy!"

Chance laughed and pulled her back. "Hold on a minute. There are conditions. Some strong ones."

"Oh." Her face fell. She'd probably have to wear a nun's habit and sing only Baptist hymns. It was just like her father to give her a little, then take away even more.

"You still have to follow all the rules we have now."

"But, Daddy! If I can't go out on school nights, how can we practice? And if I have to be home at eleven on weekends, how can we ever do a gig?"

"You'll have to practice here," he said. "I'll clean up the empty barn for you. That way I can keep an eye on you."

"Daddy, I'll *die* if I have to tell them that! They already treat me like a child—"

"You are a child. And I'm your father. They can take it or leave it."

She breathed out a despairing breath and stood up, raking her hand through her hair. "What about the gigs?"

If a moan could be shown in an expression, Chance wore it. "I'll have to approve every one of them," he said with great reluctance, "but if I do, you can go. And I put my foot down when it comes to dying your hair blue or any other color. And you don't leave this house until I see what you're planning to wear on the stage. I don't want my little girl looking like her legs are tattooed in psychedelic colors, or bopping in some miniskirt that barely covers your—"

"What is psychedelic?" Jeanie cut in.

Chance rolled his eyes. "Never mind. Do we have a deal or not?"

Jeanie shrugged. "I guess so, Daddy. The truth is, this is better than I expected. Maybe I have Simone to thank."

"Simone did her damndest to argue your case," he conceded, "but I won't say it did a lot of good. I make my own decisions where you're concerned."

Not convinced, Jeanie leaned over and hugged her father again. "Thank you, Daddy. If the band goes for it, you won't be sorry."

"They'll go for it," he said. "After tonight, there's no doubt in my mind, or theirs, that you're their ticket."

"Their ticket to where?" she asked.

He grinned and rubbed his face, leaving it red. "Hell if I know. And if it's okay, I'd just as soon not have to think about that now. Go wash your hair, sweetheart, and... congratulations. You have a lot to be proud of tonight."

Tears sprang to Jeanie's eyes and quickly she turned away and started back to her bedroom, trying not to launch into flight as she did. Her father's approval had meant more to her than all two hundred of her peers' tonight, she thought. And now he was letting her stay in the band!

She reached her room and began undressing for her shower, when it occurred to her that she owed Simone her thanks. Grinning, she looked up her teacher's number and went to her father's room for his cordless phone.

Taking it into her bedroom so that he couldn't hear, she dialed Simone's number.

"Hello?"

"Simone?" she asked, keeping her voice low. "This is Jeanie."

"Hi, kiddo," Simone said with a smile in her voice. "I figured you'd be signing autographs or recording contracts right about now. What are you doing calling me?''

''I wanted to thank you,'' she said.

''Thank me? For what?''

''For whatever you said to my dad to make him let me stay in the band.''

''He's going to let you? Really?'' She could hear the interest—and surprise—in her teacher's voice. ''Well, well. I'm surprised. I didn't think he had it in him.''

It wasn't what she said, but the tone of her voice, that alerted Jeanie to the hostility wavering just below the surface. ''What do you mean?''

''Well... he's pretty stubborn. Not that that's bad, I guess. I mean, he is your father, and I don't mean to say anything bad about him... not that there's anything bad to say... it's just...''

Jeanie frowned, trying to follow her babbling. ''Didn't you two get along?''

''Get along?'' Simone asked. ''No, not really. Well, I mean, yes... at first. Real well, in fact. Until he insulted Dino.''

''Dino?''

''My dog. He came over here and insulted my dog. Called him a urinating hippopotamus and said he needed obedience training, that I was ruining him... or something to that effect.''

The words didn't sink in as much as the realization that her father had gone to her favorite teacher's home. Had they shared a drink? Had they kissed?

Her eyes widened at the image, and an idea began forming in her mind. ''He is stubborn, all right, but most of his girlfriends overlook that because he's so handsome.''

Simone was quiet for a fraction of a second before she asked, "Most of his girlfriends? How many does he have?"

"Oh, four or five. Not any more, though. They call him all the time, but he really is available."

"Available?"

"Yes. I mean, if you're interested or something. I wouldn't blame you if you were. My dad is a real catch... according to his other ladies."

"Is that so?" Simone asked sarcastically. "Well, I take it he hasn't sat in their living rooms trashing their dogs."

"I'm sorry about that," Jeanie said. "That really isn't like him. He's just so passionate about dogs. Really, he's pretty passionate about a lot of things.... You two must have gotten along a little...."

"What did he tell you?" The question sliced through her words, startling Jeanie, but alerting her that there was something to tell.

"About what?"

"About our getting along," Simone said. "Before the talk about Dino, I mean?"

"Well... not much." She grasped for a gauntlet to throw out, one that Simone might pick up, and decided that lying through her teeth might help. "He just said that he really likes you a lot. He said you were one of the best-looking women he's seen in a long time, and that he'd like to get to know you better. Something like that."

"He said that?" Simone asked.

"Well, yeah. And he was sitting in his chair staring at a blank television when I got home. I bet he was thinking about you."

"Why would he be thinking about me?" Simone asked.

"I don't know," Jeanie said in a teasing voice. "Maybe he's got it real bad."

Simone didn't respond at all, and Jeanie knew that if her comment had had no effect, she would have come back with some retort. She hoped she had stirred just the right embers to interest the woman.

"Well . . . I've got to go wash my hair. I just wanted to thank you."

"I didn't do anything. Really. I half expected him to force you out of the band just because it made him so uncomfortable."

"But he didn't, so he must have put more stock in what you said than you thought. By the way, you two were so cute dancing together tonight."

"Uh . . . thanks," Simone said quietly.

"Yeah. Anyway, I'll see you Monday."

When Jeanie hung up the phone, she had a smile on her face and a scheme in her head.

Chapter Five

Simone hung up the phone, frowning, and wondered if it was just her imagination that the girl was trying to matchmake.

Most of his girlfriends...he's so handsome...a real catch...

A smile broke through her frown, and she realized that Jeanie had something up her sleeve.

She sat down at the table, where a bowl of soup steamed in front of her—a poor semblance of the supper she had failed to eat that night. Before the dance she had taken more pains with her appearance than usual, for she knew that Chance would be there. She hadn't planned to wind up in his arms, wondering how to gracefully shed her blouse without seeming wanton!

But she hadn't expected it to end the way it had, either.

Maybe she was too critical... too analytical... too ready to throw a man out for the simplest flaws. But she had learned long ago that her emotions were too precious to be wasted on someone unworthy of them. Too many times she had overlooked divine signals in favor of those emotions, and always her heart became a casualty. The last time had almost done her in.

It was the closest she had ever come to marriage.... So close, in fact, that the license had been applied for. For two rocky years she had endured constant criticism, negativism and Adam's almost total domination over her. But she had loved him with blind innocence and fevered passion, always looking upon his need to change her as something that she, no doubt, needed.

But that week of her wedding he had disappeared for two days, only to return to inform her that he had been thinking and that he had finally realized their marriage would never work. She was too flighty, too silly, too spontaneous. What he needed was maturity, predictability, security.

Swallowing the lump of pride in her throat, she had given him back his ring and told him sweetly that she would never forget him.

And she had kept that promise, but it wasn't the good times she remembered, only the long, lingering pain...the loss of heart...and the flattened self-esteem it took her years to rebuild. No, she had never forgotten, and the memory blocked every attraction she had had since then.

Only now could she look at herself and not feel guilty liking what she saw. She was a good friend to herself, and never again would she listen quietly while someone tried to chip away at that friendship.

No, Chance hadn't tried to do that tonight, but his criticism of her handling of Dino, and his opinions on her teaching methods, had sounded too much like

Adam's well-meaning barbs. Maybe she had overreacted.

She heard a pounding on the back door, where she had let Dino out for a while, and went to let him in. The minute the door opened the dog bolted in, once again tackling her to the floor.

"Dino!" She let out a yelped command for him to let her up, and half obeying, the dog romped over her toward the kitchen table. She had barely gotten to her feet and closed the door when she heard a crash.

Swinging around, she saw that he'd knocked one leg out from under the kitchen table and the bowl of soup she'd been eating had slid off, to crash into a million pieces.

Instantly the dog began licking up the spilled soup, despite her efforts to pull him away. "Dino, stop it!"

Red-faced, she grabbed his collar and dragged him back to the door with all her might. "Come ... here ... you ... stupid ... dog!" Her bare foot slipped on the soup and she fell down, almost losing her grip.

Quickly she scurried back up, continuing to drag the dog. Reaching the door, she opened it and with one last thrust of strength, forced Dino through it.

As if she had locked out the Beast himself, she flung her body back against the door, slid down it and sat on the floor, surveying the damage around her.

Suddenly she began to cry, and she sat there and wept for as long as she could stand, with the soup jelling on the floor and Dino hurling his body against the door, demanding to be let in.

When she had at last managed to clean up the mess and put her table back together, and after she managed to get Dino settled down for the night, she thought about the things Chance had said tonight. Maybe he was right, she thought. Maybe she was creating a monster. Maybe Dino did need obedience training, and maybe that wasn't criticism of her.

If things got any worse she might have to surrender the house to the dog completely, and she doubted he could handle the mortgage payments!

Exhausted, she fell into bed, with visions of Dino in a military uniform and Chance wearing a Hitler mustache lulling her to sleep. But at least her furniture, and her bones, would remain intact. Sometimes spirits needed to be tamed. She just wasn't sure that her own wouldn't be broken in the process.

And as those dreams shifted to Chance lying next to her in this bed, holding her and inciting fever and desire in her that she didn't know how to control, she decided she owed it to herself to see him just one more time. Maybe then she'd be able to reinforce the negatives about him more than the positives. Maybe then she would be able to find some perspective about him, and put him out of her mind once and for all.

THE PHONE RANG before Chance had even gotten out of bed the next morning. He heard Jeanie pick up on the extension in the kitchen, but he answered, "Hello?"

"Chance? It's me. Simone."

"Yeah?" he asked, straining to see the time on the clock. It was 7:00 a.m. Slowly he sat up, trying to clear the grogginess from his brain.

"I waited until seven," she said, "because I didn't want to wake you, but it was kind of urgent."

He waited for Jeanie to hang up, but realized she wasn't going to. "Jeanie . . . are you on?"

She hesitated a moment, then confessed, "Yes."

"Hang up," he said.

The phone clicked, and he raked his hand through his hair and fell back on his pillow, still clutching the phone to his ear. "Now, what's wrong?"

"It's Dino," she said. "I'm calling to eat crow, Chance. To cry uncle. You can make fun of me and say I told you so, and I'll sit stoically by and take it."

"What are you talking about?"

"I want to take your advice and sign Dino up for obedience training. As soon as possible."

Chance slid his feet to the floor and sat up on the bed. "Why? What changed your mind?"

"Let's just say Dino changed it for me. Please, don't make me grovel. Just tell me when and where."

He smiled, picturing Dino misbehaving in all sorts of ways, with Simone getting all flabbergasted and ineffectively loud. "Well, I'll be glad to sign you up, but I don't have another class starting for three weeks."

"No!" she cried. "I can't wait that long! I might not survive it!"

He laughed aloud then, but she didn't find it amusing.

"You saw him last night! You said yourself that he needs help!"

"He does, Simone, but it can wait three weeks."

He could hear the edge in her voice, but finally she sighed. "All right. Sign us up. I guess we'll make it somehow."

"Meanwhile, you can have a little more time to enjoy your dog's wonderful spirit," he teased.

She moaned. "Go ahead. Hit me again. I deserve it."

He laughed and shook his head. "A little discipline goes a long way, Simone. You'll see."

"Yeah, yeah. Whatever. All I know is that I've run out of choices."

"You always have choices."

The double meaning behind his words quieted her, and he wanted to ask her if he could see her tonight, or today, or better yet, right now, for breakfast. But he looked up and saw Jeanie, clad in her nightshirt, with her hair—her nice, plain blond hair—stringing disheveled around her shoulders.

"So...I'll get in touch with you later about when the class starts. You won't regret it, Simone."

She hesitated a moment, and he knew the chemistry between them last night was as much on her mind as his. But perhaps it was better that they couldn't discuss it. "All right, Chance. Just let me know."

He hung up and looked up at his daughter, and realized that she looked a little too excited about the call. He didn't like getting her hopes up about something that had such potential for disaster, so he decided to play it down as much as he could.

"What did she want, Dad?"

"She wanted to sign her dog up for an obedience class. We don't have one for three weeks, though—"

"Private lessons!" Jeanie cut in. "Daddy, give her private lessons. She's such a good friend, we owe her that much—"

"*Owe* her? What do I owe her for?"

"For being such a good teacher to me. For turning me around, making school fun..."

"School isn't supposed to be fun," he said, turning back to his bed and making it up as he spoke. "It's something you should take more seriously. And teachers aren't supposed to be good friends. Besides, she's no good friend of mine...."

"Well, she might be if you hadn't insulted her dog!"

He turned around, frowning at the child who had exasperated him so lately. How did she know what had happened last night? He hadn't told her.

"Jeanie, did you talk to her last night? After you got home?"

That look of innocent guilt fell over her face, and she shrugged. "Well...maybe for a minute. Just to thank her for talking to you about the band."

"What exactly did she tell you?"

"Just that," Jeanie said. "And some other stuff."

"*What* other stuff?"

He knew his face was reddening and that his reaction was a little too unchecked, but he couldn't help the anger rising up inside him.

"Just...that she likes you. She asked me about your other girlfriends and stuff...."

"What other girlfriends?"

"Just if you had any."

"And what did you tell her?"

Jeanie's grin was full of mischief. "I sort of told her that you had four or five."

Surprisingly, a grin stole across his face. "You didn't."

"I don't know why I did it, Daddy. It just came out. But I told her that I didn't think you were real interested in any of them and that you were available."

"Oh, my God, it gets worse." He raked a hand through his hair and dropped onto his bed. "Jeanie, what's gotten into you?"

As if commiserating with him, Jeanie dropped down next to him and shook her head. "I don't know, Daddy. I guess I just wanted to make you look like a stud."

Chance couldn't help the laughter erupting in his chest and he dropped his face into his hands. After a moment, he looked up at his daughter. "Jeanie, leave all that to me, will you? I don't need help in that department."

"Oooh, sounds serious," she teased, bouncing to her feet.

"It's not," he said. "Really. I want you to stay out of this. And I don't want you pinning your hopes on Simone and me getting together."

"But she's so cute, Daddy, and she told me she really likes you. You know, she has all sorts of men picking her up after school every day," she lied, "but I don't think she's attached to any of them. She seemed to really like you, though. Brian mentioned it."

"Jeanie, that woman and I have nothing in common."

"You have me in common," she said. "Besides, we're not talking about some big relationship. We're talking about private lessons for her dog. But I can understand your not wanting to be alone with her.

She's really beautiful, and it's been a long time since you've been with a woman...."

"How do you know how long it's been?" he defended, realizing even as he did that the argument was absurd. "Jeanie, it's not your job to find me a woman. I can find one for myself, if I want one. I don't need my daughter setting up dates for me."

"I'm not asking you to date her, Daddy!" She cocked her head, as if analyzing his state of mind. "You know, I think you might be protesting a little too much. That tells me there might be something there. But, hey, if you can't handle it, wait until the class starts up. You know what they say about safety in numbers."

He stared at her for a moment, wondering if she was mature and intelligent enough to snooker him this way, or if her comments were really innocent. He wasn't afraid of Simone, after all, and it wasn't like he was going to let his passion for her overwhelm him. The worst that could happen was that she would get angry again at his discipline of Dino.

The best that could happen was that the next time they might not be interrupted....

He fought back the direction his thoughts were taking and turned back to his daughter. "All right, Jeanie, I'll do it. But not because of any attraction I have to her.... Because I don't... have one, I mean. She's a nice person, and yes, she's a woman, an attractive one...."

"She smells good, too," Jeanie said. "She let me wear her perfume last night. Don't you think she smells good?"

"I didn't get close enough to find out," he lied, recalling the scent that seemed to have implanted itself on his senses. "As I was saying, I don't want you getting it into your head that anything is going to happen between us. We're not each other's type.... Not at all."

"Yeah, right," Jeanie said with a grin, and went to the phone. Picking it up, she handed it to him. "Call her now, Dad."

Feeling like a kid being urged on by a sister, rather than a father taking orders from his daughter, he took the phone and obediently dialed the number that Jeanie called out to him.

GETTING DINO OUT of the van at Chance's was like coaxing Custer out of hiding, and as much as Simone loved her dog, she wished she had the ammunition Custer faced as he took his last stand. Any other time, the dog would have bounded out the driver's door, tearing her clothes and knocking her down as he went. Today, however, he could smell the scent of discipline just around the corner, and she was sure that his dog sense told him this could, quite possibly—and hopefully—change his life forever.

"It's not going to be so bad, Dino," she said as she tugged at her six-foot-long leash, which was hooked to his leather collar. The dog didn't budge.

"It's not like military school. They don't even make you wear a uniform. And the treats...I've heard they have an abundance of treats. All you have to do is listen and obey. Please, Dino. Come...on!"

She gave the leash one final pull, putting all her weight into it, but the dog dipped his head down, allowing the collar to slip over it. Simone stumbled back and looked down at the empty leash and collar at her feet. "Darn it, Dino. I'm getting tired of this!"

"Is there a problem?"

Simone turned around and saw Chance standing behind her, arms crossed and grinning as if he was enjoying the show. She shoved her hair back out of her eyes and tossed him the leash. "It came off. I can't get him out of the van. He smells authority and he doesn't like it a bit. I can't say I blame him."

"I'll take care of this," Chance said, tossing the leash back into the van. "And that leash can stay here, along with the collar. That's one of your problems. This leash is way too long, and the collar is ineffective." Reaching into his pocket, he pulled out a small linked choke collar.

"This is what I like to use in training. It comes with the course."

Simone looked at the chain-linked collar and winced. "Won't that hurt? Besides, I promised him no uniforms."

Chance laughed and climbed into the van. "It's not a uniform, is it, boy?" he asked quietly as he put the collar on the dog. "It's a new collar. And it's infinitely less painful than that leather thing cutting into your neck."

He scratched the dog between his front legs, and slowly Dino's shaking subsided. "Simone, go inside that kennel door over there and grab the chain leash I saved for Dino. It's the first on the left."

Still not certain whether his methods were humane, Simone did as she was told and returned with the cold chain leash. "Isn't this too short? He'll drag me a mile with this."

Again, Chance laughed. "Not when he leaves my class, he won't. I'm going to teach you how to walk him on a short leash without being dragged anywhere. And he's going to be a much happier dog."

"Uh-huh." She watched as he hooked the leash onto the choke collar, then stepped down from the van. "Look, I don't want you to hurt him."

Chance ignored her and bent over to call Dino. "Come, Dino. Come on." He gave the chain a quick jerk, and to Simone's surprise, the dog jumped down instantly.

"Good dog," he said in a higher pitched voice while he scratched behind Dino's ears. He reached into his other pocket and withdrew a Milkbone. Dino snapped it up and ate it with gusto. "See what a good dog you are? Don't worry, Dino. We'll get Simone straightened out. She just needs a little training."

"Me?"

"Yes, you," he said, standing back up and handing her the leash. "I find that the owners often need more training than the dogs do. You didn't think you were just going to drop him off and let me 'fix' him, did you?"

"Well, I..."

"Sorry. We're in this together. All three of us." Again, he scratched Dino, making his tail wag frantically, and grinning at the worried look on Simone's face, he handed her the leash. "The first thing I'm going to teach you is how to hold a leash the right way. And whether Dino has faith or not, I know before the day's over, you'll be in top form."

Simone took the leash reluctantly, feeling a little like a woman who had been committed to an institution that she thought she was taking a friend to. But who was she to balk at bizarre teaching methods? She wrapped the chain links around her hand—just before Dino thrust forward, pulling her off her feet.

BY THE END of the two-hour session, Dino was walking at Simone's side without dragging her on her stomach, he was sitting when told, he was no longer jumping on her, and he was grinning and panting like an overgrown puppy who knew he deserved a scratch behind the ears.

Simone, on the other hand, was defeated. Earlier, she had feared that Chance would be mean to Dino, but instead she had watched him pamper and scratch and reward the dog.... While he never ceased to humiliate, embarrass and scold her for doing everything wrong. She hadn't held the leash right, she hadn't used the right tone of voice to call Dino, she hadn't rewarded him enough, she hadn't punished him properly, she hadn't walked right. In her wildest dreams, she had never expected to need obedience training worse than her dog. Idly, she wondered if her ex-fiancé had set up this whole charade.

Chance noted her somber mood, and grinning, took Dino's leash from her hand. "Stop pouting. You'll get your reward yet."

"For what?" Simone deadpanned. "I haven't done one thing right. The animal rescue league will probably come out any minute to take Dino away from me. How he survived this long is beyond me."

"Oh, you didn't do any worse than any other dog owner does. I told you, it's usually not the dog that needs work as much as its owner."

"Oh. So now I 'need work.' I don't know how you've stood being around me all afternoon."

"It wasn't so bad," he teased. He walked Dino to a small fenced-in area and removed his leash. Dino took off across the grassed yard, frolicking as he had always done. "See, no broken spirit there."

"Yeah," she said with a smile. "And no broken dishes or furniture..."

"Or moods."

Not missing the reference to the other night, Simone matched his grin. "I guess you're right. A little control never hurt anyone."

He leaned over and whispered in her ear, "Whoever told you that was an idiot."

She felt the heat climbing her face, and knew he could see it.

"Come on," he said, taking her hand. "Let's go in and get something cold to drink. Then we can check out Jeanie and the band. I like to pop in every now and then just to remind them that I'm here."

She tried not to concentrate on the feel of his hand around hers, so big and callused and virile. And she tried even harder not to think about his reference earlier to the "broken mood" of the night they'd been together. She merely fell into step beside him. "Sounds good to me. And I'm still waiting for my Milkbone."

IN THE BARN, the band made it all the way through their newest song for the first time, and Brian did a showboat run on his guitar and sidled up to Jeanie.

"The other night at the dance, it was so cool when we were doing the same steps, and it looked like we'd planned it that way," he said.

Jeanie grinned. "Yeah, I know. We ought to really plan some steps and do that every time."

"You, me and Joe-Joe could really get down," he said. "We could give it this...." He did a rocking sidestep, shoving her into the step with his hip, until she picked up and joined him. Joe-Joe, plucking his bass guitar, tried to imitate them. "My sister used to do this crazy dance called the Bump. We could jazz it up a little and bring it back."

"I wouldn't mind bumping butts with your sister," Neal, the drummer, threw in. "Hey, what's happening with her and your old man, Jeanie? I saw her driving up earlier. Are they an item or what?"

"Not yet, but I'm working on it," Jeanie said. "I think my dad likes her. He gets all defensive whenever he talks about her."

"Really?" Brian asked. "Simone gets all flustered and red-faced when she talks about your dad. We might just be on to something here."

"Yeah," Neal said. "Maybe if they start hanging out together, it'll get Jeanie's old man off our backs."

Jeanie's smile faded, and she turned around. "He's not on our backs. He's just being a father, that's all."

"Well, my father doesn't check up on me every hour on the hour," he said. "Damn, it's like he thinks we'll rape you or something if he leaves us alone."

Brian grinned. "Maybe he's just got your number, Neal."

Neal grinned and picked up the beer he had stuffed into a paper sack.

"My father trusts me," she said. "He just worries."

Neal took a swig of his beer and chuckled. "I don't know, but I don't think I could handle that kind of dictatorship in my house. My old man treats me like an adult—"

"My father treats me like one, too," she said. "But this is hard for him."

"And you honestly think he won't mind you bumping butts with Brian on the stage?"

"Shut up, Neal." Brian's outburst startled Jeanie, and she realized that this was getting more tense than she had intended. "We came here to practice, not to make sleazy comments about each other...or even Jeanie's father. We're practicing in the best place we've ever had, thanks to him, so just shut up. It's his barn, and if he wants to look in on us sometimes, what's the difference?"

"The difference is that we're not little kids. At least, not all of us."

Tears sprang to Jeanie's eyes, and she looked down at her feet.

"We have a song to rehearse," Brian said through his teeth. "Do you think you can handle that, man?"

Neal's devil grin faded, and he picked up his drumsticks and did a short roll on his cymbal. "Let's go," he said.

The song started up again, but this time Brian didn't dance with her. This time, he stood still, his eyes cast down at the concrete floor, his back rigid as he played the song without any feeling.

Jeanie tried to sing her best, despite the fact that she felt she had unknowingly driven a wedge between the members of the band. The worst part was Neal's adamance in treating her like a kid...and his animosity toward her father. But there was nothing she could do to change things.

She only hoped that somehow Simone would shift her father's attention away from her, and that he would make his presence around here a little less apparent when they were practicing from now on.

BUT CHANCE HAD other plans, and after he and Simone had made a pitcher of lemonade and finished off two glasses, they walked across the lawn to the barn where the band was practicing. From outside, they could hear the slow song drolling out, and Chance paused before going in.

"Is that 'Tupelo Honey?'" he asked, listening.

Simone smiled. "So that's why Brian stole all my Van Morrison albums. He said they wanted to incorporate some 'oldies' into the show. Is that Brian singing?"

Chance listened a little longer, then nodded. "Yeah, with Jeanie singing harmony. That's nice."

He reached down, took her hand and pulled her against him. "Let's dance."

"Out here? In broad daylight?"

"It's not broad daylight. It's dusk. Besides, who am I to mess with a mood once it hits?"

She slid her hand up to his shoulder and took his hand and he pulled it against his chest and began to dance.

She smiled up at him, and smelled the scent of lemonade on his breath. "You're a great dancer."

"You're no slouch, yourself," he said.

He took her hand and spun her, and she came back into his arms, giggling like a teenager. "I wasn't expecting that."

"That's the way I like it," he said. "Keep 'em guessing."

He spun her again, and this time she came out of it more gracefully. She couldn't help grinning up at him in anticipation and he asked, "What are you grinning about?"

"You," she said. "I don't know what you'll do next."

"What do you think I'll do?" he asked.

Before she could answer, he dipped her, and she dropped her head back, giggling. "You drop me and I'll hurt you."

He pulled her back up and spun her again, then spun himself. When their eyes met, they were both laughing.

"This is fun," he said, drawing her against him again. "I like dancing with you."

"The song's almost over," she said. "Do you think they'd play it a couple dozen more times if we asked them?"

"I don't know," he said. "We could tell them that it really stunk and they need a lot of practice."

"No. My brother would never believe that. He'd see right through it and think we just wanted a reason to dance."

"Do we have to have a reason?" he asked, grinning.

"No, I don't guess," she said. "Do we have to go in there? Couldn't we just stay out here without their knowing it for a little longer?"

"Sounds good to me," he said.

The band launched into the Mariah Carey tune that Jeanie had dedicated to them the first time they had danced, and Chance grinned and pulled her against him again. "I think they're playing our song."

Smiling, because she couldn't help herself, Simone let him sweep her around, and wondered if he had any idea that he was sweeping her off her feet at the same time. But somehow, she thought he did know, for he slowed his step and held her tightly against him, and she looked up at him and realized that he was going to kiss her. She felt herself floating suddenly, as if she were weightless...as if she could fly away on a breath.

Their lips met, and he touched her face, stroking it as his mouth played sweet, sultry games with hers, and she rose up on her toes and curled into the kiss. He was strength and softness at the same time; he was security and adventure; he was safety and danger; he was kindness and madness.

And as she let herself drift into that madness, she realized that she was taking a risk she hadn't taken in years. She was falling without meaning to, and she didn't have a safety net. She only hoped that the broken places from the last fall had healed stronger, and that this time, she wouldn't wind up shattered.

But whether she did or not, she thought, she had no choice, for Chance Avery had taken all her choices from her.

THEY NEVER MADE IT into the barn to "check up" on Jeanie, but instead went back to the house, where Chance said he had boiled some shrimp earlier that day. They had to eat, he said, but Simone knew that it was only a pretense for their being alone. It was a pretense she didn't mind at all.

When they reached his kitchen, he picked her up and set her on the counter and poured some shrimp cocktail sauce into a bowl. Then, taking a shrimp out of the pot and dipping it into the sauce, he leaned against her knees and teased it in front of her lips. "Here," he whispered. "Taste this."

Her heart tripped into a dangerous rhythm, and she opened her mouth and took a bite. He watched her as she chewed, and finally she got a shrimp of her own, dipped it and held it up for him to eat.

She had never imagined chewing to be a particularly sensuous act, but today it had a meaning all its own. She found her mouth going dry as he moved his around the shrimp, and when he reached up to dab a spot of sauce from her lip, she swallowed and waited, holding her breath.

As she had hoped, as she had prayed, he leaned over and kissed her again, but this time it was with an urgency that couldn't be denied. This time, it was with a hunger that shrimp couldn't sate. This time, it was with a craving that would drive them both mad if they didn't find a way to quell it.

He opened her knees and slipped between them, and pulled her closer. She closed her arms around his neck and fell, dizzy, into the kiss, allowing him to support her with his strong, probing hands moving around her back.

And then those hands moved between them and she felt him pulling her shirt out of her jeans, felt his warm calluses against her ribs, felt the excitement of his fingers moving upward.

The kiss grew more hurried, more fervent, more frenzied, and when he slipped his hand beneath her bra and cupped her breasts, she breathed a moan and deepened the kiss even further. His breathing was ragged as he broke the kiss and pulled up her shirt, unclasped her bra and dipped his face to kiss the nipples that swelled and ached and peaked.

"I want you," he whispered. "Just being with you today has driven me crazy. Ever since we didn't finish what we started the other night—"

"I want you, too," she breathed. "But this is insane."

"I know," he said. "Jeanie could come home any minute."

"And we barely know each other. It's too soon."

"I know," he said. "I know."

He touched her breasts again, circled the aureole with a finger, then finally, with trembling hands, pulled the bra back to cover them. "You're a very sexy lady," he whispered. "And I think I'm gonna have a real hard time sleeping tonight."

She pulled her shirt back down, and shaking, tucked it back in. Disappointment edged through her, but she knew stopping had been the best thing. That realization did nothing to quiet her screaming hormones, however.

She slid off the counter and looked up at him. "Why don't we go outside?"

"Where it's safe?" he asked with a lazy grin.

"Where it's cool," she said. "Where we can talk, and not get quite so tangled up...."

He took her hand and pulled her out of the kitchen, through the living room, and out the front door.

By now, the sky had faded into blackness and was beginning to sparkle with its first few stars. Chance went to the porch swing and pulled her down next to him.

"I really should be getting home," she said. "It's late, and I didn't mean to stay so long. This two-hour lesson turned into several extra hours, didn't it?"

The moonlight angling down cast half of his face in shadow, but she could see the gentle sparkle in his silver eyes. "I came up with every idea I could for getting you to stay longer," he whispered. "Trouble is, we can't carry out the best idea of all."

"It's way too soon," she whispered again. "I'm not the kind who can be intimate with someone I've just met. It goes against the grain."

"Me, too," he said. "I really don't usually get that carried away. You just do something to me. You make things fun. Even fighting with you the other night had an element of fun."

She gave him a wry look. "I don't quite know how to take that."

He smiled. "You know what I mean. You have a very special spirit about you. You're different. I'd be willing to bet that you never have a dull moment."

"I have a lot of lively ones," she admitted, "but I have my dull ones, too. Sometimes it's not much fun being lively all alone."

"I know the feeling." His eyes met hers, intensely searching deep inside her, waiting for something she didn't know whether she could give. She stared back at him, her big eyes wondering, watching, waiting.

"You have very pretty eyes, do you know that?" he asked quietly.

She blushed and told herself she was too old for such childish reactions. "Thank you."

"No, really. I'm not just saying it. You have very sweet eyes. Eyes that say a lot about what's inside you."

"When I first met you, you didn't much like what was inside me."

"I didn't *know* what was inside you," he said. "I just knew what I thought was. I've learned a few things today."

"So have I," she whispered.

Again, that crackling silence stretched between them, a silence that was wonderful in its promise, a silence that was frightening in its uncertainty.

He moved his hand from his face and gently stroked her hair with the tips of his fingers, as he continued to hold her gaze.

Finally his fingers pressed gently against her head, as his face moved infinitesimally closer. "We shouldn't kiss out here on the porch, where Jeanie could see us if she came out," he whispered.

"I know," she said. "That's why we came out here, isn't it? To keep us apart."

Their lips hovered millimeters apart for a moment, as their eyes probed for some sign of negation.

Then slowly, as if they had never expressed their need to keep their distance, or the importance of not being seen, his eyes fell to her mouth, then closed as he grazed her lips with his own.

The kiss set off a small explosion in her heart, and she felt the sparks seething through her bloodstream.

She moved her hands up his chest, to his shoulders, and let her fingers feather through the softness of his hair.

Their lips grew wetter as the kiss intensified, and she parted her lips slightly, allowing him sweet entrance. Something jolted in her heart the moment their tongues met, and she felt his arms closing around her....

As she melted again into his kiss, she savored the feel of his arms enveloping her with security and strength. They made her feel small and protected. He tasted of shrimp cocktail and lemonade, but they tasted better in the warmth of his mouth than they had when she had eaten them herself.

Again, he worked her shirt out of her jeans and touched the bare skin of her ribs. That hand slid upward, upward, and she caught it before he reached her breast. "Chance..."

"What?" he asked, and she saw how smoky his eyes were in the moonlight.

"We can't. We really can't."

He pulled back, unable to alter the heaviness of his breath. "I know," he whispered. "I...I didn't really mean to do that. Or any of this."

Instead, she only looked up at him. His eyes looked stricken as they locked with hers, and suddenly, before she realized it was happening, he had taken her back in his arms and claimed her lips again. This kiss was deeper, harder, more urgent, and her heart pounded in a runaway rhythm as she lost herself within it. Across the yard in the barn, a sweet, slow love song droned across the night.

He pulled back and gazed down at her. "Now, that I meant to do," he whispered.

She smiled. "You kiss as good as you dance."

"It's been a long time...."

"Yeah," she said. "For me, too."

"No. I don't believe you."

She laughed softly. "Why not?"

"Because," he said. "A woman like you... you must have men standing in line to ask you out."

"I don't go out with everyone who asks me," she said. "And the ones I do go out with, well, if they don't light my fire, I don't usually wind up kissing them."

Instantly she regretted her choice of words, for it was a confession of emotions she was better off not expressing. It also sounded childish, she told herself.

"Light your fire, huh?" he asked with a grin. "You only kiss men who light your fire?"

She felt that heat creeping up her cheeks again. "I only kiss like that when someone lights my fire."

"And what happens when your fire gets lit?" he asked, his face growing serious.

She felt herself growing hot, uneasy, and clearing her throat, she smiled down at her hands. "I don't know," she said. "It's been a long time."

A too palpable quiet passed between them, during which she could have sworn she heard her own heart beating. Desperately she wanted to look up at him, touch his face and guide his mouth back to hers. But would he misinterpret that? Would he think "lighting her fire" meant igniting something she wasn't ready to accelerate yet?

"Look, I didn't mean... I mean, I don't want you to misinterpret what I just said... or what just happened...."

The hope on his face fell, and he shook his head. "No, me either. I don't want you to think..."

"What?" she asked, looking up at him.

"Well, you know."

"Yes," she said, not at all sure they were talking about the same thing. "I know. We don't want this to..."

"Get out of hand," he prompted.

She nodded. "Yes, that's what I meant, too."

"I mean, I have enough problems trying to raise Jeanie."

She frowned, and suddenly realized that just maybe they *weren't* talking about the same thing. She had been afraid of his misinterpreting her "lit fire" as being ready to jump into bed. But what *was* he saying?

"Well... of course, you do."

"Yeah," he went on, looking as uncertain as she. "And... and the last thing I need is to get serious with someone like you."

Her backbone stiffened, and her expression faded. "Someone like me?"

"Yes. I mean... well, someone who's so different... who has such different ideas on child rearing."

"Wait a minute!" She came to her feet, letting the swing rock with the release of her weight. "I'm talking about necking with you, and all of a sudden you're talking about raising kids? Are we on the same wavelength?"

He stood up and slid his hands into his pockets, the look on his face telling her that he wasn't sure *what* they were talking about. "Well...yes. My point was that we probably aren't all that compatible...that we shouldn't let a little chemistry get out of hand...."

"Good," she said, not sure it was good at all. "Because that's just what I meant. It shouldn't get out of hand. That child-rearing stuff kind of sounded like—"

"I just meant that I'm not ready to get into anything serious. Just in case you made more out of it than I did."

Her ego felt bruised, even though she didn't quite know what had struck the blow. Trying to salvage her pride, she lifted her chin. "I agree. The last thing I need right now is to be an instant mom. I'm not really mother material."

"You're telling me," he said.

The absolute certainty in his voice struck her like a five iron across her forehead, and she stepped back, staring at him. She felt mortifying tears coming to her eyes, and determined not to let him see them, turned away. "I'll go get Dino," she said. "I need to get home."

"Simone. You don't have to leave yet."

"Yes, I do," she said.

He followed her to the gate and watched her slip Dino's new choke collar back over his head. "Simone, did that make you mad? What I said?"

"Why would it make me mad?" she asked, not looking at him.

She took the dog and started walking out to her van, and Chance followed close behind. "Well...I don't know. You just don't look real happy."

"I'm great," she said, opening the van and letting Dino jump inside. Slamming the door, she turned back to him. "It's been fun...as well as educational," she said. "I'll see you the next session. And next time I won't stay so long."

"What? Why not? Simone, I didn't mean to make you mad. I was just—"

"I know what you were doing," she said, opening her door and stepping up into her seat. "You were just making it clear that just because we got a little hot and bothered, it didn't mean you were really interested in me. You wanted to make sure that I didn't have illusions of hooking the confirmed bachelor on the basis of a physical attraction."

"I did not mean that. Well...maybe I did in a way, but not in that way..."

She cranked her engine and slammed the door, and looked out at him through the open window. "You've got a lot of nerve," she said. "What in the world makes you think that I'd be so bowled over by you? What in the world makes you so damn sure that I'd be the least bit interested in any kind of relationship?"

"Well, excuse me. I thought we enjoyed each other's company today."

"So did I," she said with fire in her eyes. "My mistake."

With that, she rolled up her window viciously, and drove away.

For the second time since he had met her, Chance stood out in the drive staring at her disappearing tail-lights and wondering what in the world he had said to make her so mad.

Chapter Six

"Great, Dad. You did it again, didn't you?"

Chance turned around and saw Jeanie standing in the drive behind him, her arms crossed and disapproval written all over her face. Back at the barn, the band members were loading their instruments into their cars.

"Did what?" he asked, annoyed.

"You made her mad. What did you say, Dad? Did you insult her dog again?"

"No, I didn't insult her dog. Dino and I got along just fine."

"Then you insulted her. Dad, when are you going to learn how to get along with women?"

The authoritative tone in her voice would have amused him, if it hadn't been so accurate. "I get along just fine with women. She's a little overly sensitive, that's all. She takes things the wrong way and twists them around. . . ."

"Oh, Dad," Jeanie said, shaking her head and starting toward the house, as if washing her hands of him once and for all. "You're absolutely hopeless."

Chance stood, flabbergasted, as one more woman walked away from him.

THE BED SEEMED HARDER than usual, and Simone couldn't get comfortable. She tossed and turned, wishing for the power of sleep that Dino seemed to have as he lay in his bed at the corner of her room.

But it wasn't the bed that kept her from sleeping tonight, she realized. It was Chance. Chance and his flirtatious instruction today. Chance and his kiss. Chance and his insults.

The phone rang, startling her, and she looked at the clock and saw that it was after midnight. Praying it wasn't an obscene call—probably from a student who got a kick out of frightening teachers—she picked it up.

"Hello?"

"Did I wake you?"

Chance's deep voice was unmistakable, and raising up on one elbow, she shook her head.

"No."

"Come on, it's after midnight. I know I woke you."

"Well, if you were so sure I was asleep, why did you call?"

He paused for a moment, thinking. "I...I don't know, really."

"You don't know?" She sat up fully, clutching the phone to her ear, and tried to understand.

"Yeah, I don't know. I just felt like you were mad at me when you left. Like I'd said something wrong."

"So I was mad," she confirmed. "What difference does it make?"

"I don't know," he said. "But for some reason it makes a difference to me."

She plopped down flat on the bed, still holding the phone, and stared up at the ceiling. "Look, Chance, it's nothing personal. You say things that set me off, I say things that set you off.... We just rub each other the wrong way."

"Not always," he said. "We didn't rub each other the wrong way when we were eating shrimp. And when we were dancing. And when we kissed."

"Yeah, well, things changed, didn't they?"

"Yeah, they did," he said. "And I know why. It was because I opened my mouth and stuck my foot in, sock, shoe and all, and said something insensitive that I didn't even mean."

She sat up again, as if to hear him better, and frowned. "What are you talking about?"

"I honestly didn't know at first," he went on, his voice a soft, deep rumble. "But I've thought about it for hours, reliving every word, and I finally figured out that it was the crack about motherhood that did it."

"Well, I'll admit it didn't give me a good, warm feeling."

"I know it didn't. I was out of line. But if you remember, you said it first. I just agreed."

"I know you did," she said on a heavy sigh. "You agreed, and that told me a lot. Some people just aren't meant for each other, Chance, even when there's a physical attraction. You were right."

"Right about what?"

"About our not getting serious. I'd like to take that even a step further. I think we shouldn't get involved at all. We'd be wasting each other's time."

"Would we? How do you figure that?"

"Because we have fundamental differences," she pointed out. "I think I'm a terrific person, and you don't."

He chuckled softly, and the sound sent goose bumps tickling over her skin. "I do think you're terrific," he said. "A little unorthodox at times, but...besides, those aren't fundamental differences. Fundamental differences are important things like an atheist dating a priest...."

"Or a father dating someone who isn't mother material."

"No. I told you, I didn't mean that."

She sighed and shook her head, feeling a sudden emptiness deep within her that she didn't quite know how to quell. "It doesn't matter, Chance. It really doesn't. I'm who I am, and you're who you are."

"And never the twain shall meet?"

"Something like that."

There was a long moment of silence, and finally Chance spoke again. "Well, I guess I'll let you go."

"Yeah," she whispered. "See ya."

"See ya."

For a moment, they both lingered on the phone, neither willing to hang up first. Finally Simone took the phone from her ear and dropped it into its cradle.

CHANCE CUT OFF the lamp and dropped back into his bed, feeling more aggravated than he had before he had called her. Why had he insulted the very essence of her womanhood—her maternal instinct? Why had he allowed his mouth to be so insensitive? And why couldn't he ever say what he meant when he was around her?

She didn't want to see him again, and he couldn't say he blamed her. Still, he couldn't stop thinking of her response to his kiss, of the way she had moved against him, of how small she had felt in the circle of his arms, of how agonizingly his body had reacted to her. He felt his groin stirring in response to the memory, and he cursed himself for cutting the moment so short. How long had it been since he had held a woman? Too long, he told himself. Way too long.

He turned over and punched his pillow, and tried to push thoughts of her out of his mind. She had gotten under his skin somehow, and that scared him to death. But what was worse was the knowledge that it didn't even bother her if she never saw him again. Damn it, he thought, it wasn't supposed to happen this way. He was supposed to be in control. He was supposed to decide when it was time to call it quits.

But damn it, he wouldn't grovel, and he wouldn't call her again. If the woman couldn't accept a simple apology, then he wasn't going to extend it again. He was better off without her. Neither he nor Jeanie needed a third party in their lives, after all. They had done just fine until now.

THE ACTIVITY IN the hall at school was almost deafening the next day, as Simone cut through the crowds waiting for the bell to ring. She saw Jeanie coming toward her and quickly looked around for an escape route. But it was too late.

"So you didn't get much sleep, either, huh?" Jeanie asked as she met Simone and turned to walk the rest of the way with her.

"I slept fine. What makes you say that?"

"Because you have those bags under your eyes. Just like Dad."

"Your father has bags under his eyes?" she asked. "Good. He probably deserves it."

"Look, whatever he said to you, he didn't mean it. He has this problem with saying things he doesn't mean. And the fact that he called you in the middle of the night—"

Simone stopped and turned around, frowning at the girl. "Jeanie, how did you know he called me last night?"

"I heard him," she said. "I'm a light sleeper."

"Well, then you know that we didn't end on the best note."

"But that could change," Jeanie argued. "Come on, Simone. My dad really likes you. I know he does."

Suddenly it occurred to Simone that Jeanie had more of a stake in this than she had originally given her credit for. She was trying to fix them up, and that was all the more reason for Simone to cut things off. "Look, Jeanie, don't get any ideas here. Your father and I are friends... Not even friends, really. We're acquaintances. That's all. We're not compatible in any way, and whatever you think might happen between us, you're wasting your time. I don't plan to see him again. Period."

"What about your obedience sessions?"

"*Dino's* obedience sessions," she said, chagrined that everyone assumed *she* was the one who needed the training. "Your father was very helpful to me yesterday, and I think I can take it from here. I don't really see any point in continuing."

"Oh, boy, he really said something awful, didn't he? What was it, Simone?"

"Nothing!" she said. "Just leave it alone. I appreciate the fact that you think I'd be good for your father. Really, I do. I think it's sweet that you would have singled me out that way, but there's no chance of anything happening."

She waited a second, while Jeanie tried to summon some more arguments, but when it was clear that the girl was coming up empty, she shrugged and tugged on a strand of Jeanie's hair. "I've got to get to class now."

Jeanie caught her breath and as Simone started away she shouted, "That doesn't change the sleepless night you both had. That's something in common, isn't it?"

"I told you, I slept fine!" Simone threw back before disappearing around the corner.

JEANIE THOUGHT ABOUT the dead end she had hit with her father and Simone for the rest of the day, and that afternoon, when she ran into Brian, who claimed to be looking for his sister after school, she seized the opportunity to talk to him about it.

"I really thought they were getting along," she mourned, as they sat across from one another at the picnic table in the campus courtyard.

"So did I," he said. "I know my sister. She gets that look in her eye when she's around him. It's kind of silly, but I know what it means. She hasn't had that look in her eye since Adam."

"Adam? Who's he?"

"The guy she almost married. Real hard-nosed dude. Always giving her a hard time, and she always just took it. Then one day, he just kissed her good-bye. Practically left her at the altar. She hasn't really trusted anybody since."

"Gee, that's sad."

"Yeah," Brian agreed. "The saddest part is that he worked for a company that made video games. When she stopped seeing him, I had to start paying for those suckers."

Jeanie grinned. "I meant sad for Simone."

"Yeah, right. That, too," he said. "'Course, it's not like we haven't all tried to get her interested in romance again. She dates now and then, but she goes out with these nondescript, no-personality Milquetoasts who wouldn't know romance if it came up and kissed them. And then, just the other day, on her birthday, I hired this guy—"

His voice stopped short, and he began to giggle under his breath.

"Go ahead. Hired him for what?"

Brian wiped his grin and cleared his throat. "To strip."

Jeanie gaped at him. "You hired a stripper to take his clothes off for Simone?"

"It was just a joke," he said. "Joe-Joe and I got a good laugh. Ol' Mrs. Seal across the street had something to talk about for a while, too, I'd imagine. . . ."

Waving her off, he changed the subject. "Anyway, I think Simone really has the hots for your dad."

"Then why won't she talk to him? Why is she cancelling her lessons?"

"Stubborn," he said with certainty. "My sister is the most stubborn woman alive."

"And so is my dad. See? They'd be great together."

They laughed, and finally Brian leaned forward on the table. "How did they meet, anyway? Maybe that would give you an idea of how to get them back together."

"My father came up here to yell at her about me being in the band."

"Then you were the common denominator," he said. "Maybe that could work again. Maybe you could do something that would make your father come up here again."

The spark in Jeanie's eyes was contagious. "Yeah. That could work."

"What can I say?" Brian asked with a grin. "I'm a genius."

They laughed again, and finally Brian told her he had to leave to get ready for rehearsal that night. It didn't occur to her until he was driving away in his car that he hadn't found Simone. The truth was, he hadn't really even looked for her! Could it have been that he had really come there to see her?

The thought sent a wave of exhilaration through her, but she told herself not to get her hopes up. There was a lot of potential for disappointment in her life right now, and the last thing she needed was to set herself up for it.

Instead she drew her thoughts back to Brian's suggestion. Something to make Chance approach Simone again...It had to be something just drastic enough to shake her father up, and open some communication between him and Simone again.... Suddenly the idea came to her.

An ecstatic smile curved her lips as she rushed out to her car, determined to get things going before the end of the day.

"OH, MY GOD, what have you done?"

That evening, Jeanie grinned at her father and struck a pose, showing off the side of her head that had been shaved a few inches above one ear. "What do you think? Isn't it great?"

"You shaved your head," he said, his expression still unchanging. "You *shaved* your head!"

"Not all of it," she defended. "Just the side. It's cool, Daddy, and it'll fit right in with my new image. I need to look different to be onstage. It makes me look—"

"Like a crazy woman," he finished for her, still gaping at the shaved spot on her head. "Jeanie, what got into you to make you do a thing like this?"

"Well, gee, Daddy. It's not like it's permanent. It'll grow back in a few months."

Chance rubbed both hands down his face, leaving red finger streaks. "I can't believe you did this. Who in the world gave you an asinine idea like this, anyway? Was it someone in the band? Did they tell you you had to do this?"

"No, Daddy," she said quickly. "No one in the band has even seen it yet. They'll be surprised. The truth is, this was Simone's brainstorm. I think it's a great one, don't you?"

Fire blazed in Chance's eyes, and he wadded the roots of his own hair. His voice was violently quiet as he asked, "Are you telling me that that woman told you to get your head shaved?"

"Just part of it, Daddy! Geez. It's not like I'm completely bald!"

Chance shook his head. "I can't believe I'm having this conversation with my little girl."

Jeanie giggled. "I'm not a little girl, anymore, Daddy. I'm becoming a woman."

"A woman with a shaved head." He went to the telephone, grabbed the book and began flipping through the pages for a phone number.

"What are you doing?" Jeanie asked, as if she didn't know.

"Looking for that woman's number," he said. He jerked up the phone and punched out the number, and Jeanie could have sworn she saw smoke coming out his ears as he waited for her to answer.

But Simone wasn't home.

Slamming down the phone, he cursed. "What kind of person doesn't have an answering machine?" he muttered, flopping the phone book closed. He looked up at his daughter and pointed to her. "You go to your room."

"Why? I didn't do anything wrong. I'm allowed to get my hair cut like I want to."

"You know better than to do something so drastic. We *talked* about this."

"We talked about dying it, Daddy, not shaving it."

"I'm going to that school first thing tomorrow," he said, "and by God, I'm going to take care of this.

That woman has influenced you for the last time. Now go to your room."

Jeanie tried not to grin as she followed her father's orders, for he was following her plans to a T. Tomorrow he would storm up to the school, confront Simone, she would deny telling Jeanie anything, and the next thing she knew, they'd be madly in love and planning a life together.

Of course, it would mean big-time punishment for Jeanie, but she would figure some way out of it. Besides, if her father was in love, he'd be in a good mood, and he'd be a little easier to get around. She only hoped her plan worked, because if it didn't, she might be the one to regret it the most.

Living with this hairstyle would be bad enough, but living with it confined to her room for the rest of her teenage years would be more than she could handle. Her only consolation was that it would, eventually, grow back out.... And if it did the job for which it was intended, it would be worth every agonizing moment.

Chapter Seven

The final bell rang out through the school corridor like the opening bell at a boxing match, and as dodging students were rushing out of the classrooms, Chance made his way to Simone's class, expecting to find her in some ridiculous costume shouting out cues to her pupils. Today, he thought, he could demonstrate the use of the guillotine himself.... On her! He almost looked forward to the confrontation.

But Simone wasn't there.

Frustrated, and not willing to be foiled in his anger, he rushed to the office and leaned over the counter separating him from the secretarial desks. "Excuse me. I'm looking for Simone Stevens. Do you know where I could find her?"

"I think she's gone home already," the secretary told him. "I saw her car pull out just after the bell rang."

Silently Chance cursed and raked a hand through his hair. "All right, then. Is the principal in? I need to talk to him."

"Yes, he's in," she said. "May I tell him what it's about?"

"It's about Miss Stevens," he bit out. "I'd like to file a complaint against her."

AN HOUR LATER, Chance discovered that his level of agitation had not been helped by filing the complaint. It had only made him more aware of the things he had against Simone. The principal had taken copious notes, had asked a hundred questions, and had seemed intent on doing something about the problem.

Chance hoped she got the lecture of her life, he thought, as he cranked his car and started out of the parking lot. He hoped she got her hand severely slapped. He hoped she would be shaken into not interfering in her students' lives anymore.

Telling his daughter to shave her head! What would be next? Psychedelic tattoos? An earring through her nose?

The further he drove, the madder he got, and finally he realized he was not heading home, but was driving in the direction of her house. He couldn't be sure that the principal would confront her, but he damn well could do it himself.

Her van was home, so he pulled into the drive behind it. Urgently he banged on her front door.

Simone answered it in seconds, with Dino barking behind her. Recognizing Chance, the dog jumped up on him and slapped a huge tongue up his face.

"Down, Dino," he said. "I taught you better than this."

Dino cowered down and sulked away.

Simone gave him a haughty look, but didn't invite him in. "Yes? May I help you?"

"As a matter of fact, you can," he said. "But can I come in, or would you prefer to have this out in front of all your neighbors?"

"Have what out?"

She stepped back and let him in, and he brushed past her. When the door was closed, he swung around, hands on his hips, and faced her with fire in his eyes.

"How could you do it? After all I've said to you, after all we've talked about?"

"Do what?" she asked, growing more annoyed with each word.

"How could you tell my daughter to shave her head?"

"Shave her head? Her head wasn't shaved. I saw it today. It's just one side, and—"

"Her head is shaved!" he shouted, aching to throttle her. "How could you tell her to do that, when you knew how I felt about it?"

"Wait a minute!" she bellowed, effectively shutting him up. "I did not tell your daughter to do any such thing, so don't you dare come in here and start accusing me."

"She said you told her."

Simone gaped at him, her face distorted as she tried to understand. "Why would she say that? I haven't even had a personal conversation with her in days, and not once about her hair. Are you sure she said *I* told her?"

"Positive," he said. "Why would she lie? She knew I'd storm over here and have it out with you."

The realization of Jeanie's intention dawned slowly over Simone and her anger faded.

"Maybe that's exactly what she hoped for."

"What do you mean?" he asked.

"I mean, maybe that was her plan. Chance, I'm beginning to think we've been had."

Still unable to grasp her meaning, he squinted and shook his head. "I don't—"

"She was trying to get us talking again," she said. "I think Jeanie nurses some secret fantasy of our getting together as a couple. She might have set this up, hoping to get us talking again."

He stared at her for a stricken moment, then dolefully rubbed his forehead. "Oh, my God. Is she really that smart?"

"Teenagers have very conniving minds," she said with a slow grin.

"Well, then, is she that brave? She must have known this would fall back on her."

"Maybe it was worth it to her," she said quietly.

Chance gave her a softer look, packed full of apology. "I...guess I was out of line. You really had nothing to do with this?"

"No, Chance," Simone said. "I would never have done that. I could have guessed how you'd feel about it, just like she guessed."

"Damn, she's got her old man figured out," he said, dropping down onto her sofa and combing his fingers through his hair. "When did I get to be so predictable?"

"I suspect it's evolved over the years," she said, sitting down next to him.

He smiled. "I have been cursing you all night long. I stormed up to the school looking for you...."

"I came home so I'd have some quiet to grade papers," she said.

He looked at her fully, his soft eyes probing into hers. "I'm really sorry," he said. "I shouldn't have leapt to conclusions. I should have realized. . . ."

"It's okay," she whispered.

For a moment they stared at each other, and finally Chance laid his arm across the back of the couch and shifted around to face her. "Maybe Jeanie was on to something," he whispered, "although I'd never admit it to her."

"On to what?" she asked.

His eyes dropped to her lips, and unconsciously she wet them. "Finding a way to get us talking again. It worked."

She didn't answer, as his lips descended to hers. His kiss was startling in its hunger, and she realized that he had thought about it a lot since the last night they were together, as well. Her heart pushed those doubts out of her mind, doubts about what he had said about motherhood; doubts about how different their outlooks were on life, in general; doubts about the things he had said that he hadn't meant to say.

Somehow, as the kiss deepened, as their hands caressed and stroked and explored, as he tightened his embrace and held her as if she belonged to him, she stopped thinking and felt, instead.

When the kiss broke, he looked down at her, his breathing hard and his hands trembling slightly. "I'm sorry I hurt you the other day," he whispered. "I didn't mean it. I ramble sometimes, say things that I haven't thought out. . . ."

"Me, too," she whispered.

He didn't release his embrace of her, and she thought that if he did, she might not be able to stand the sudden contrast from belonging to loneliness.

"I'm really sorry about today, too," he said. "Blaming you. Accusing you."

"We were set up," she said. "Jeanie planned it all that way."

"Yeah, but I shouldn't have gone off so half-cocked. I shouldn't have filed that complaint."

Her face changed instantly, and stiffening, she looked up at him. "What complaint?"

"With your principal," he said. "But don't worry, I'll go take it all back."

Alarm flashed through her eyes. "You filed a complaint with my principal? *Today?*"

"Well . . . yes, but we can get it all straightened out. It's no big deal."

"No big deal?" She flung herself out of his arms and stood up, facing him like an executioner. "Chance, how could you do that to me? You have no idea what this means!"

"Simone, I told you I'd straighten it out. I was mad. My temper got the best of me."

"No!" Her face burned as she glared down at him. "Your temper got the best of *me!* I could lose my job over this." Her eyes filled with tears and her mouth twisted with the effort of holding them back. "You don't know what you've done."

He stood up, suddenly aware that she took this much more seriously than he did. "Simone, even if you *had* told Jeanie to cut her hair, you wouldn't lose your job over it. I expected them to slap your wrist, and that's all."

"Oh, they'll slap my wrist, all right." She covered her face with a trembling hand and closed her eyes. "Just leave," she said. "I'm sorry, but I don't have anything to say to you anymore. Please, just go."

Chance stood before her for a moment longer, staring in helplessness, searching for something to say to clear him of this weight she had hoisted onto his conscience. Finally, when he realized she couldn't be swayed, he walked to the door. "Simone, I really didn't intend to hurt you."

"Well, you know what they say about the road to Hell being paved with good intentions."

Still not quite sure what horrible crime he had committed, Chance left her standing there, knowing the hurt in her eyes was deep, but not having a clue how to fix what he had broken.

WHEN JEANIE SCREECHED into the driveway after school the next day, with tears raging down her face and an expression of despair and fury—reactions that he was sure had nothing to do with the fact that he had grounded her the day before for lying to him about Simone—Chance found out why what he had done was so wrong.

"Daddy, how could you go to the principal? She might lose her job because of me!"

"What?" He pulled Jeanie into the house and closed the door, and stared down at his daughter. "She might lose her job over a stupid haircut?"

"It wasn't just the haircut," Jeanie said. "A lot of parents and some of the teachers are out to get her. This was just the final thing they needed to nail her!"

She clutched her head and wailed. "Oh, it's all my fault."

"You shouldn't have lied, Jeanie. You tried to manipulate me, and it got out of hand."

"I know, and I told them, Daddy. But no one would believe me. They said I was just covering for her because I like her. That all the kids like her because she's an irresponsible teacher."

"Oh, my God." He dropped down into his chair and covered his face with his hands. "I never meant for it to go this far. I was just mad."

"Oh, Daddy, you filed a written complaint. That always means something. She's the best teacher I've ever had. If they fire her, there's no justice in this world. None!"

Chance sat silent as he watched Jeanie run out of the room, slamming doors behind her. For a moment he sat still, letting the thoughts reel through his mind. Thoughts about his temper yesterday, about his getting even, and then about how hurt Simone had been when she had found out. She had known what his actions would mean. No wonder she had thrown him out.

He had been all wrong, he told himself, and now he was responsible for jeopardizing her career. Unable to bear it, he got up, grabbed his car keys and headed for the school, hoping Mr. McCall would still be there. It wasn't too late to set this right, he told himself. And if it was the last thing he did, he would make sure Simone didn't lose her job.

"BUT I TOLD YOU it was all a mistake!" Chance shouted moments later, when he stood before the principal's desk. "Damn it, my daughter lied to me. I was acting in haste, without knowing all the facts!"

"It isn't just you, Mr. Avery," Jack McCall said, cleaning his glasses with a handkerchief as he spoke. "We have lots of other complaints. And even if I did disregard what you said about her yesterday, you also told me about her influencing your daughter into dying her hair blue, getting into a rock band, dressing like a heathen...."

"Jeanie's sixteen. She's learning how to express herself. Simone hasn't done anything to hurt her."

"That's not how you felt yesterday, Mr. Avery," he said, putting his glasses back on. "Yesterday, you wanted me to reprimand her."

"Reprimand her, yes. Fire her, no!"

"No one said she would lose her job. That's up to the board."

"But don't you see how wrong it is to have a hearing to determine whether she'll keep her job, based on wrong information that I gave you?"

"No, Mr. Avery. This is something I should have done a long time ago. I let Miss Stevens talk me out of it, but I warned her if I had one more complaint, we'd have to do something. Yesterday, you levied three. I think those could prove she's interfering in her students' lives, undermining their parents and displaying an alarming amount of mind control. That kind of thing can be dangerous, and I want to put a stop to it. Now, if you'll excuse me, I have work to do."

Cursing under his breath, Chance left the principal's office, racking his brain for a way to save her from this mess he had created. Damn it, why had he done it? How would he ever face her again? And how would he face his daughter?

Knowing that somehow he had to come up with an answer, Chance drove home sorting out all the possibilities.

THE BAND MEMBERS weren't due to show up until 4:30, but Jeanie went to the barn early to escape her father's mood when he returned from the school. She was still angry at him, but even more outdone with herself. They had both made a mess of Simone's life, and neither knew how to undo it now.

She opened the barn door, expecting to find it empty, but the sight of Brian sitting on a stool in the corner startled her.

"Hi," she said. "You're early."

"Yeah. I came to talk to you."

Something in her heart flipped, and a bud of hope sprouted inside her. "What about?"

"About what you did to my sister."

Her heart collapsed like a lead weight dropped from a thirteen-story building, and she cleared her throat. "I don't blame you for being mad. I only did it to get my father talking to her again. I didn't know how it would turn out. I never thought—"

"That's just it," Brian said, sliding off the stool and facing her. "You didn't think. When you go accusing her of things she didn't do, there's a lot more at stake than a couple of dates with your father."

Tears burst into her eyes. "I was stupid," she admitted. "I tried to undo it today, but they wouldn't listen. Even Daddy talked to Mr. McCall. I don't know what else to do. Tell me what to do and I'll do it."

"It's too late, Jeanie," he said. "The damage has been done. All we can do now is hope that the board is a little kinder to her than you were."

He left the barn then, and she dropped her face into her hands and cried out her misery, her self-deprecation, and her regrets. And as much as she hated herself for what she'd done, she knew there was nothing she could do about it now.

LATER THAT NIGHT, darkness invaded the living room like a live being, creeping into Chance's soul as he sat in his recliner, staring at the flashing television. It was only nine o'clock, and already Jeanie was sound asleep in her bed. He wondered when the last time was she'd gone to bed that early, and decided it had been years. But she'd been burning the candle at both ends lately and she'd been as depressed over Simone as he. She seemed to want to be alone, and he couldn't blame her.

Selfishly, he wished she'd stayed up longer, for he didn't like this feeling of desolation. Loneliness wasn't something he'd allowed himself to dwell on very often.

But that was before he'd spent an evening laughing and bantering with Simone. That was before he'd held her and kissed her. That was before he'd destroyed her.

He looked at the phone, and Simone's number flashed through his mind. He couldn't call her, he thought. What would he say? She probably hated him by now. She had probably hired a voodoo witch to make a doll of him. At this very moment, she was probably spearing it with a hairpin.

But something about the hurt in her eyes when she realized what he had done, told him that she wasn't the vindictive type. Maybe she would listen to him. Maybe together they could work something out.

He picked up the telephone and dialed her number, and waited, with his breath held, as it began to ring.

THE MOMENT THE PHONE rang, Dino began a wild race with her to get it, as if he expected it to be for him. When she picked it up, he jumped up on her, forgetting everything he'd learned the other day, and she stumbled back and caught hold of the sofa arm.

"Dino, down!"

At least that worked, she thought, for Chance had taught her the proper tone, and Dino had had his choke collar jerked just enough times to make him want to obey. Silently she breathed out relief.

"Hello?"

"Simone? It sounds like a three-ring circus there. Everything all right?"

Recognizing Chance's voice, she sighed and sat down. "Yes. Everything's fine. It was just Dino."

"I told you he'd need a few more lessons for it to stick."

She looked at the dog, sitting anxiously on the floor with his tongue hanging out, his tail thumping behind him. "No, thanks. I can handle it."

"All right," he said quietly. "I can't say I blame you." Another moment passed, and finally he cleared his throat. "Look, Simone, I don't even know how to tell you how sorry I am for what I've done. I reacted too quickly, and if I'd known what was at stake I never would have done what I did."

Simone dropped her forehead into her hand and shook her head. "I accept your apology, Chance. Now, if you'll excuse me, I was in the middle of something...."

"Simone?"

She stopped midsentence and paused, sincerely not wanting to hear any more. It was asinine that she could still be attracted to and mooning over a man who had hurt her in such a big way. "What?"

"I really wish...I wish things had turned out differently.... With us, I mean. I like you a lot." He cut himself off, and she heard him whisper a curse away from the phone, as if the effort of expressing himself was too painful.

She smiled softly.

"I would like to help you, if I only knew what to do. I'm going to see if I could testify at your hearing. I could explain how my complaint was a mistake...."

"It wouldn't help," she said dolefully. "There are too many others. I've been a target for a couple of years now, and the little things are just adding up. It had to come to a head sometime."

"Still, I'm going to try," he said. "And I'm not through trying to figure out other things I can do to help. It's not over yet, Simone."

"I appreciate that."

She wished there was something more she could say, but there really wasn't anything. For the first time in her life, she was at a loss for words.

"Well...I won't keep you any longer," he said. "I just...wanted to talk to you.... Tell you how sorry I am. If you decide you want to finish the course with Dino, we can do it anytime. And I won't charge you."

"Yeah, thanks," she said.

He paused for a moment longer, and finally she heard him sigh. "Well, good night."

"Good night," she said.

She hung up the phone and sat back on the couch, and as the tears pushed into her eyes, she curled her legs up beneath her and told herself it was going to be a long night.

IN HER BEDROOM, Jeanie wiped the tears from beneath her eyes and stared down at the phone she'd brought into her room. She had been holding it for over an hour, trying to gather the courage to call Brian and smooth things over, but she doubted it could be done.

Still, the need to talk to him, to at least try, forced her to dial the number, and trembling, she held it to her ear.

"Hello?"

It was Brian, and it took a moment for her to find her voice. "Brian?"

"Yeah?"

She swallowed and sat up, trying to make herself sound less broken. "This is Jeanie."

Silence was her only answer, and she burst into tears and pinched the bridge of her nose. "You hardly spoke to me at all during rehearsal today, and I can't stand this. I don't know how to tell you or Simone how sorry I am for what I did. It was stupid, and I hate myself...."

"Don't cry." His words cut into her confession, and she caught her breath and wiped her tears. Quickly, others rolled down her cheeks. "I never meant to make you cry."

She tried to calm her voice, but it was too shaky. "Brian, I really like you, and I don't want you to hate me. Simone doesn't even hate me."

"I don't hate you," he said with a heavy sigh. "The truth is, I don't even really have the right to blame you. I just found out today that I might have done her more harm than you did."

"What?" she asked. "How? What did you do?"

He was quiet for a moment, and finally he said, "Remember that stripper I told you about? The one I sent to her house for her birthday? Well, Mrs. Seal, one of the members of the school board, came in and saw him. Now that's one of the complaints that's been brought against Simone." His voice dropped to a barely audible pitch, and he whispered, "So you can stop beating yourself up. I had no right to come down so hard on you when I'm as much to blame."

"How could you have known that Mrs. Seal would see him?" she asked, in a feeble effort to console him.

"The truth is, I didn't really care. I just wanted a good laugh." He took a deep breath, then began again. "The horrible thing is that she isn't even mad at me. I'd feel so much better if she'd curse at me or scream and yell or something."

"I know," Jeanie said. "She's just trying to punish us. It's all so selfish."

Together, they laughed, and finally Jeanie said, "The truth is that Simone doesn't have a selfish bone in her body. That's why I like her so much. That's why I was trying to move mountains to get my dad and her together."

"Maybe you should just let those mountains move themselves, Jeanie. Maybe I should, too."

"Yeah," she whispered. "At least you're not still mad at me. Are you?"

"No," he said. "I'm not mad. I really like you, Jeanie. I wouldn't have stayed mad for long, even if you hadn't called. But I'm glad you did."

"Yeah," she whispered. "Me, too."

Later, as she lay in her bed staring at the ceiling, she thought of Brian and the gentle words he had whispered over the phone.

And as she drifted off to sleep, she was determined to find a way to make things right for him . . . as well as his sister.

Chapter Eight

"I'm glad you got some extra rest last night," Chance told Jeanie over breakfast. "You needed it."

Jeanie picked at her food, still unable to eat. "Yeah. I feel a little better now."

"This thing with Simone has been getting to me, too," he said, stabbing at the sausage he'd fried with the eggs. "I'll admit I've lost a little sleep over it. And she really didn't want to talk to me last night...."

"You called her last night?"

Chance looked up at her, and realized he shouldn't have admitted that. She would get her imagination revved up again, and who knew what she'd do next? "I called her to apologize. That's all, Jeanie. I feel real bad about what I did."

"And what did she say? Did she accept?"

"Of course, she accepted. She's a classy lady."

"But?"

He grinned at his perceptive daughter and shrugged. "But she really didn't have much else to say to me. Which was fine. That was all I called for."

"Oh." Disheartened, Jeanie began to tear her toast into little pieces.

Chance watched her, wondering how transparent he really was to his daughter. Did she know just how much this thing with Simone had affected him? Could she see that he had spent way too much time thinking about her lately?

He cleared his throat and tried to look down at the newspaper, as if what he was about to say was offhand. "You know, maybe you could get some of the students together. Start a campaign of some kind."

"Me?" Jeanie looked up at him, frowning. "What do you mean?"

"I mean...well, you know...start a petition... write some letters. Talk to the principal. Paint a few signs. Let the school board know how important she is to you."

Slowly the light dawned in Jeanie's eyes. "That's a great idea. I'll bet every one of her students would help. We could stage a protest...a walk-out.... We could hold some rallies...."

"Hold on," Chance said. "I don't want anyone else getting into trouble over this. No broken rules, okay? If you do something wrong, it's going to fall back on her. Don't cause any trouble. Just make yourselves heard in a peaceful, legal way, and I'll be behind you a hundred percent."

"Whatever we do, it'll have to be soon," Jeanie said, quickly taking her empty plate to the sink and rinsing it off. She turned around and grabbed her books. "Her hearing's in just a few days, you know."

"No," he said. "I didn't know they had scheduled a date."

"They have. And the rumor around school is that Mr. McCall has already been interviewing teachers to take her place."

"Aw, hell," he said. "They don't waste any time. You do what you can from your end, and I'll go pay another visit to him today. If nothing else, maybe they'll let me speak at the hearing."

Jeanie bent down and pressed a kiss on her father's cheek. "Thanks, Daddy."

He grinned and watched his daughter prance away.

CHANCE WAITED UNTIL the school day was almost over before he paid a visit to the principal, hoping he might catch Simone on her way out. Once again, he sat in Mr. McCall's office, stomach knotted, and tried hard to reason with the man who paced across the room with the door open, as if he could only spare a moment of his time before he would flit away on another errand.

"This just isn't right. I heard you were interviewing her replacement already. Whatever happened to innocent until proven guilty?"

"I'm not condemning her already," the man said. "I'm simply preparing for a worst-case scenario. It isn't easy to be in my position, you know. I have a job to do, no matter how distasteful it may be."

"And you figure it's going to be distasteful? As in firing an excellent teacher?"

The principal reluctantly plopped into his chair and steepled his fingers in front of his face.

"Look, Mr. McCall, the grades of her students must be a matter of record. Don't they make consistently good grades in her classes? I know my daughter's grades have improved in every subject since getting into her class."

"Of course, her students' grades are higher, Mr. Avery, but that doesn't mean it's because she's a good teacher. It could simply be *why* she's so popular. She's an easy *A*. Besides, her moral values are being questioned here, and the fact that she's inflicting her personal values on her students."

"People are jealous because she's young and pretty," he said. "That's the bottom line. When you have a good-looking single teacher on staff, the other teachers start gossiping and the parents start feeling threatened. But I know Simone Stevens, and she has the highest of values. And she's smart, especially when it comes to kids. She's already helped me tremendously in understanding my daughter."

"So much that she went out and shaved her head?"

"Hey, that's between her and me, and it has nothing to do with Simone," Chance defended.

Behind him, he heard a knock on the door and turned around to see Simone standing there. He wondered how much she had heard.

She gave Chance a cursory glance, then turned her tired, dull eyes back to her boss. "I had a message that you wanted to see me."

"Miss Stevens, I'll be with you in a few minutes, if you'll just wait out there."

Simone didn't budge. "You're discussing me, again, aren't you?"

"As a matter of fact, we are," McCall said. "Mr. Avery was just listing all the reasons he finds you attractive...."

"The hell I was..." Chance blurted.

"None of which is a recommendation to you as a teacher of any competence."

Chance came to his feet and leaned over the principal's desk. "I can't reason with you, Mr. McCall, but I can damn sure reason with the other board members. Put me on the list of people to testify and I'll tell it to them."

The bell rang, a loud, deafening peal, and the principal stood up and set his hands smugly in his pockets. "I find it very interesting that you've changed your tune so suddenly, Mr. Avery. After all, you are the one who started all this."

"I told you, my daughter lied to me. That's a problem that I have, but it has nothing to do with Simone."

The principal turned away and peered out the window, where the students should have been rushing out of the building on their way to their buses and cars. Today, all was silent. Frowning, Mr. McCall turned around.

"Didn't I hear the bell?"

Simone stepped further into the room and looked out the window. "Yes, it rang. Where is everybody?"

"I'll look in the hall." Mr. McCall went into the outer office, followed by Chance and Simone, and looked through the glass walls into the main corridor.

"The hall's empty, too. Why isn't anyone going home?"

"Maybe there's a short in the bell system," Simone offered. "Maybe they didn't hear it."

Before he had had time to absorb that possibility, a group of teachers hurried into the office. "Mr. Mc-

Call, I think you should see something," one of them said.

"Did you hear the bell?" he asked.

"Yes, we heard it. Everybody heard it."

"Why isn't anyone going home?"

"Come with us and you'll see."

Realizing for the first time that what was happening had some significance, whether it had anything to do with him or not, Chance followed Simone and the others into the corridor. Looking up it, he saw hundreds of high school students sitting on the floor, legs crossed, quietly blocking the way.

And Jeanie sat in the front row.

He caught his breath as he approached her, but the look on her face was so purposeful, so serene, that he stopped himself just short of reacting openly. He watched, astounded, as Jeanie stood up from the front row and handed the principal a clipboard with several pages attached. Then, without saying a word, she sat back down.

Mr. McCall glanced over the pages and shot Simone a daggerous look. "It's a petition," he said. "To save your job. Was this your idea, Miss Stevens?"

"No!" she said. "I didn't know anything about this. What's going on, Jeanie?"

"We're protesting," Jeanie said quietly. "We think it's unfair that you might lose your job, and we wanted to let the administration know how we feel about it."

Chance grinned and gave his daughter a wink, and she smiled. Simone's eyes misted over, and Chance saw from her poignant expression that somehow this gesture began to make up for the wrong he and Jeanie had already done to her.

"Oh, kids," she said, "that's really sweet, but—"

"I want this hall cleared out immediately," the principal said. "I'm going to count to three. One, two, three!"

Jeanie stood up then, and began clapping her hands and chanting, "Miss Stevens isn't leavin,' Miss Stevens isn't leavin'...."

All of the others, from the front to the rear of the hall, and those still standing in the classrooms, began clapping and chanting, as well.

The protest went on for an hour or more, during which the principal called the police, who politely told him that the kids weren't breaking any laws. The six o'clock news team made it to the scene before it was over, and interviewed several of the students who told how they felt Simone was being railroaded. Finally, when Mr. McCall was ready to pull every last gray hair out of his thinly covered head, Jeanie gave the signal that it was time to break up the group and go home.

Before it was even five that day, the school was empty, but the students had made their point.

THE HEADLIGHTS COMING up the long drive toward his house that night made Chance abandon the dogs he'd been playing with and walk toward his driveway.

The moment he realized it was Simone's van, his heart raced into triple time. He stepped toward the house, waited until she pulled to a halt beside the cars of the band members who were tuning up in the barn, and watched her get out.

"Hi," she said, coming toward him.

"Hi." The word came out a little too packed with emotion, so tempering his voice, he said, "I didn't expect to see you."

"Is Jeanie here?" she asked.

Chance nodded toward the house. "She's just doing the dishes before she goes over to band practice."

Simone gave him a look that cut through to his heart, a look that made him want to pull her against him and make everything better. "I'd like to talk to both of you, if that's all right."

"Sure," he said quietly. "Come on in." He slid his fingers into the tight pockets of his jeans, as if he couldn't trust them not to touch her, and led her into the house. They found Jeanie in the kitchen, and when she saw Simone, she caught her breath. "Simone! What are you doing here?"

Simone set her big, floppy purse down on the table and leaned back against it. Her smile was soft, gentle, and so sweet. Her eyes misted over, and he felt his own stinging with the effort of holding his emotion at bay.

"I came to thank you," she said, her voice shaking like the edges of her mouth. "Both of you. You, Jeanie, for getting the students to act on my behalf today, and for taking it just far enough without making it into more trouble. And you, Chance, for going to Mr. McCall today. I heard a lot of what you said, and . . . well, it was kind of a pleasant surprise."

"Why?" Chance asked. "Why would any of what I said surprise you?"

She looked down at her feet, and he saw the color blushing up her cheeks. "I don't know. I just . . . Sometimes I'm used to more enemies than allies."

"And you thought I was an enemy?"

"Of course, she did, Daddy. What else would she think?" Jeanie asked, wiping her hands on the dish towel. "We both did her in, didn't we?"

"You didn't do me in," Simone said. "If you could see the list of complaints against me... It's pretty awe-inspiring. Your complaint is just a drop in the bucket."

"But what kind of complaints could there be?" Chance asked.

"Oh, you name it. There was a girl in one of my classes who thought she was pregnant, and when it turned out to be a false alarm, I kind of had a talk with her about birth control. And I gave her the name of a doctor where she could get the Pill. Her parents found out...."

She dropped her eyes to her feet again, sighed, and went on. "And then there was the little guy who kept getting beat up, and I suggested he take up karate. He did, and when he broke the bully's arm, his parents blamed me. And, of course, there are countless complaints from the other teachers, because the kids seem to be having too much fun in my classes. They've accused me of not teaching my students, of having daily parties or something.... The list goes on and on.... You know the kind of things. You've made the same types of accusations."

If there had ever been a moment when Chance hated himself, it was now. "Simone, I'm really sorry."

Tears sprang to Jeanie's eyes, and she stepped toward her. "Me, too, Simone. I never meant to start all this. I was scheming, and I know better...."

Simone's smile was weak. "I know, sweetheart. That's why I came to thank you. That was real sweet what you did today. It meant more to me than anything that's happened in my career."

She reached out and drew Jeanie into her arms, and Chance longed to step into the embrace. But he kept his distance, and kept his hands jammed firmly in his pockets. "It was easy," Jeanie whispered. "Everybody loves you. We don't want to lose you. I just feel like such a heel. If I hadn't been trying to get you and Daddy together..."

She caught herself, as if she hadn't meant to confess to her motivation, and Simone met Chance's eyes. For a long, sizzling moment, he thought he saw longing in her eyes, as well. He thought he saw need and yearning and desire. But he couldn't be sure.

"Aren't you supposed to be at band practice?" Simone asked Jeanie.

Jeanie nodded and wiped her eyes again. "Yeah. They're probably waiting for me."

She gave her father a kiss on the cheek, and squeezed Simone's hand again. "I'm not finished yet, Simone. I'm going to think of some more things the students can do—peaceful things—that can convince the school board how important you are."

"Thanks, honey," Simone said quietly.

They watched Jeanie leave the house, then locked into each other's eyes. The pain in hers touched Chance's heart, and he wanted more than anything to wipe that pain away. But it wasn't so easy when he had put it there himself. "Are you sure you're all right?" he asked.

"Yeah," she whispered, but he could see that she was on the verge of letting her tears go. "I'm great. Really."

Tipping his head, he stepped closer and gazed down at her. "You're worried, though, aren't you?"

As if she couldn't bear to be close to him, she pushed off from the table and stepped across the room. "Yeah, I'm worried." When she turned back to him, her eyes were bright and glazed with tears. "You know, I've wanted to be a teacher since I was six years old. I had this terrific first-grade teacher, and I just learned to love school so much. I wanted to be just like her."

Chance leaned back on the counter and folded his arms, and watched her rake her fingers through her roots. Would she run, if he reached out and pulled her against him? Would she cry out her pain on his shoulder, or would she lock her emotions away from him, for fear that he would do them more damage? Unable to find an answer, he did nothing.

"Some people are called to do what they do, you know?" she went on. "Like God put a stamp on their foreheads and said, 'You, you're a teacher.' That's how it is with me. I've never wanted to be anything else. I'm good at it; I know I am. I love what I do, I love my students, I love making a difference in their lives, I love giving them a love of history and the events shaping our world today...."

Her voice broke off, and she slid her hand from her hair back down her face and covered her eyes.

"What am I going to do if they tell me I can't teach anymore?"

Something inside him snapped, and unable to keep his distance a moment longer, he reached out and took her hand, and pulled her into his arms. She didn't pull away or lock up her emotions or lash out against him. Instead, she clung to him with too much strength, and suddenly it hit him how much he had wanted to feel her in his arms again. How much he had thought about her. How much he had yearned...

He felt her crying softly against his shirt, and he dropped his face into her hair and kissed her crown. "Shh. It's okay. You're gonna be fine. They won't fire you."

"They might," she cried. "They might, Chance."

"You just have to fight," he said. "I'll help you. I'll be at that hearing, and I'm gonna fight like hell for you. You can count on that."

She looked up at him, stricken at the promise in his tone, and tears rolled down her face as she whispered, "Why?"

"Because of all the reasons you just said," he whispered, his mouth inches from hers. He stroked her wet face with his thumb, and combed his fingers through her hair. "Because I think it would be a crime for them to dismiss a teacher who has such heart. And because...because I care about you.... Because I can't stop thinking about you... and I don't like to see you hurting."

When his lips met hers, it caught them both by surprise, but she softened even more and curled into him, accepting his sweet expression without pulling away. He deepened the kiss, and his heart felt her response in the way she held him tighter, the way she raised up on her toes to meet him halfway, the way her face moved with the rhythm and dance of the kiss.

After several moments their lips broke apart, their faces still close together. "We shouldn't do this," she whispered.

"Do what?" he asked, grazing her wet lips.

"This...get involved. We shouldn't..."

"Why not?" he asked breathlessly. "Give me one good reason."

"Jeanie," she said without hesitation.

"Two good reasons," he whispered. "Give me two good reasons."

A tiny smile crept across her lips, and she gazed up at him. His eyes smiled, as well, but his lips were preoccupied with the divot at the center of her chin.

"I mean it," she whispered. "If we get involved, it'll hurt Jeanie when we break up."

"You're right," he whispered, but his arms holding her tighter and his tongue teasing the column of her neck belied his words.

His ministrations made her shiver, and she felt a heated yearning growing from her very core and rising up to color her face. "Really, Chance. It isn't a good idea. I don't want to hurt anyone.... Least of all Jeanie."

His lips fell to the opening in her blouse, and he swept his tongue deeper down, until it grazed the upper swell of her breast. She shivered again.

Their hips pressed together, and she felt the swell of his desire against her, telling her that there was more than just a kiss involved here, that this could lead further...and when it did, there would be no turning back for her. She was beginning to think about him too much already, daydreaming and fantasizing. Her emotions were tangled in those fantasies, dangerously entangled, and if those fantasies were ever played out...

He released the top button of her blouse and dropped his face further, until his tongue stroked under the fabric of her bra, making her nipples ache and bud for his touch.

"Really, Chance," she whispered without much conviction. "Don't you think this is a bad idea?"

"No. I think it's a very good idea."

"But—"

"Shh," he whispered, looking up at her again. "It'll be all right. We'll keep it all a secret. We'll see each other without telling her.... And if it doesn't work out...nobody will be hurt."

"Nobody but me," she whispered.

"And me."

Somehow, the acknowledgment of his own vulnerability heightened her desire, and she found his lips again and matched the passion he had shown her already. His hands moved over her, down her hips, pulling her harder against him.

"Jeanie will be gone for several hours," he whispered.

"I know."

"It's been a long time since I've been with a woman," he said. "A very long time."

Her breath shuddered against his ear.

"But I want you..."

"I want you, too," she whispered.

His mouth found hers again, sealing the consent that she had so mindlessly given. Closing her eyes, she savored the taste of his tongue sweeping over her lips and teasing into her mouth, the smell of the night wind on his face, the feel of the stubble on his jaw.

He lifted her up, and she slid her hands around his neck, knowing that already they had crossed the threshold of control, that already she was hopelessly lost in him, that already she had given herself away in a way that she knew could cause her pain later. But all that mattered now was quelling the pain her heart felt, the pain for which there was only one balm, the pain that had only grown and intensified since the day she had met him.

He took her to his bedroom and pushed the door closed with his shoulder. One lone lamp shone in the corner of the room, casting the room in more shadow than light. He let her feet slide down to the floor, and touched her face with a gentle hand. His eyes made love to her, while at the same time they offered her the chance to change her mind, the chance to flee before their entanglement grew more knotted.

But already their silhouette was one, reaching across the bed in anticipation of what was to come. As if following the shadow's lead, Chance laid her down on the bed and anchored her with his body.

His passion escalated as he kissed her again, and she felt his selfless selfishness as he unbuttoned her blouse, his anxious patience as he slipped it off her shoulders, his maddening sanity as he unclasped her bra and pulled it off her arms.

She saw the control snap within him, and a soft, rumble of a moan escaped his throat as his warm hands moved over her breasts, feathering lightly as he cupped them in his hands, then lowered his face to taste and suckle and send her into a delirium of wonderful agony.

Desperate for the feel of his chest against hers, she fumbled for the buttons of his shirt and wrestled it off him. Their movements grew frenzied, crazed, reckless as he pressed his bare, hair-covered chest against her swelling breasts.

His hand slid up her leg, beneath her skirt, and he discovered the silky scrap of panties beneath it. His fingers teased inside the elastic, making her arch and shiver, and finally, as if he couldn't bear the hindrance any longer, he pulled the panties down her legs, slipped her skirt over her hips, then stepped out of his own jeans.

As if their bodies had each been expressly created for the other, they came together, his arousal as urgent as her own. And as they joined, she encountered the deepest burst of relief and fulfillment she had ever known in her life. It was the relief of fantasies fulfilled, the fulfillment of relief given freely.

They soared together faster and farther than either of them had dared to dream, then fell back to earth, panting and pulsating and clinging to each other with a desperation that seemed even greater after the bond they had forged making love.

And as she surrendered to herself, to him, and to the emotions that had driven her since she had met him, she told herself that everything would be all right. Chance would see to it.

She, herself, would see to it, for giving herself to him meant loving in a way she hadn't loved in years. It meant risking.

And she was ready to take that risk.

Chapter Nine

Despite all that had happened at school that day, and the way Simone's problems should have kept Jeanie's mind busy, her phone call to Brian loomed in her mind like a tape playing over and over and over. She couldn't shake the memory of the sweet, gentle way he had whispered, *I like you, too, Jeanie.* A tiny bud of hope bloomed in her mind—hope that his feelings were more than friendship. Her head told her to take it slow, not to assume anything. But her heart had ideas of its own.

Unlike most days, when she was the first in the barn for rehearsal, today she lagged nervously at her house—dreading, yet anticipating, the moment of seeing him again. When she finally made herself go in, as the keyboard and guitars twanged into tune, Jeanie tried not to look at Brian. Surprisingly he pounced on her.

"You were great today, Jeanie. Simone told me what you did, and I saw it on the news. Man, that was ingenious!"

"Thanks. It turned out pretty well."

"Pretty well?" Joe-Joe asked. "Man, you couldn't have planned it better if you'd tried."

"A sit-in," Stevie crooned. "Just like my folks used to do in the sixties. I'll bet Ol' Man McCall's blood pressure reached an all-time high."

"He wasn't a happy camper," Jeanie said, "and the truth is that I don't know if it had any effect on things at all. But we made our point, I think."

The door opened and Neal ambled in, late as usual, carrying a can of beer in his hand.

"You're late, man," Brian said. "Where were you?"

Neal took the last swig from his beer can, crunched it in his hand and burped. "I was promoting us. I got us a gig, guys. Tonight. At the biggest club in town. The Yankee Dime."

"What?" Brian squinted and shook his head. "That's impossible. They get the biggest names in town. What would they want with us?"

"Their band canceled at the last minute," Neal said. "I got a call from the manager, who just happens to be my cousin. I had him drop by at the dance, and he heard us playing. He thinks we're good enough to fill in. Oh, and by the way, there's money involved. A third of the door take. And we don't have to break down and set up. The band left all its equipment still set up."

"All right, man!" Stevie said, turning on his keyboard and doing a run with his fingers. "That'll give us some rehearsal time."

"Man!" Joe-Joe said. "A paying gig. Man, this could take us somewhere. Not like those little high school dances."

"Wait a minute," Brian said, refusing to budge. "We *can't* play at the Yankee Dime. Jeanie's not even old enough to get in."

"Besides," she added weakly, "my father would never let me."

"'My father would never let me,'" Neal mocked. "Do you guys hear that?"

"She's right, man," Brian said. "Her father would never let her go."

"Well, she can sneak out. It has to be done."

Jeanie looked helplessly at Brian, and his face grew two degrees redder.

"I don't want her lying to her father. We get caught, and he'll make her get out altogether. We're not going."

"Correction," Neal said. "I'm going, and Joe-Joe and Stevie, they're going. And whether either of us likes it or not, you're going. *She* can stay the hell home if she wants to."

"If it weren't for her singing, we wouldn't have been asked to play in the first place," Brian shouted. "I don't recall anybody calling to hand us gigs before she was in the band. They sure didn't ask for the drumming."

Neal lunged at Brian, and Brian parried his punch and knocked him down. Stevie started yelling, and finally Jeanie shouted above all of them. "Stop it! I'll go! I'll sing at the club!"

Joe-Joe pulled Brian and Neal apart, and panting, Brian turned back to her. "You can't do that, Jeanie. We promised your dad."

"I'm not a kid," she said. "I'm a member of this band, and I'm not going to hold you back. If we have the chance to do a professional job, then we can't turn it down. We just can't."

"So what are you gonna do? Sneak out? Lie to your father?"

"Yes," she said defiantly. "It's the only thing I *can* do. I won't get caught."

"But, Jeanie—"

"No more discussion," she said. "If we're playing there tonight, we have a lot of work to do."

As Brian reluctantly picked up his guitar and the band began warming up, Jeanie tried to push her conscience out of her mind. She was in too deep to quit now, she thought. All she could do was pray she wouldn't get caught.

"I'D BETTER LEAVE or we'll get caught," Simone whispered against Chance's neck as they lay, still entangled, beneath the covers in Chance's bed. "Jeanie could come back anytime."

"As long as we can hear the music, we're okay," he said.

She smiled. "I guess that's not a bad philosophy, is it?"

"No, it isn't." He kissed her again, long and deep, and with the same lingering fever warmth that he had had before they made love. Stroking her hair back from her face, he whispered, "I don't want you to go."

His eyes, mirror silver, reflected the adoration in her own. "I don't want to, either," she said, "but I really don't like taking chances."

"I've got it all figured out," he said. "If Jeanie came in, I'd hear the front door. And I'd get dressed and go out and act like I was alone."

"And what about my van? You know she'd see it."

"I'd tell her you were in the kennel playing with Spooner."

Simone smiled and propped herself up on an elbow. "You *have* thought about this."

"It's part of being a single parent," he said, with a grin. "You find yourself always thinking twenty steps ahead."

"And trying to cover your tracks?"

He grinned and nuzzled her neck. "I rarely have any tracks that need to be covered."

Laughing, she slipped out of his arms, grabbed her clothes, and began to pull them back on. "Well, you do now, Chance."

"You've corrupted me," he teased.

She slanted her head and squinted at him. "Who's corrupting whom?"

Grabbing her, he wrestled her back down on the bed. "I guess it's equal."

He kissed her again, and she melted once more and lay, relaxed, beneath him. "I really have to go," she said.

"I know," he whispered. "When can I see you again?"

"Soon."

"How soon?"

"When do you want?"

"Tonight?"

She smiled. "It already is tonight."

"I know," he said. "But it's just barely dark. I meant that I'd like to take you out somewhere tonight."

Her smile grew even more effervescent. "What will you tell Jeanie?"

"That I'm going to watch football with a buddy. I won't be back late, and she'll probably be practicing late, anyway. We can go out. How's dinner and dancing sound?"

Exhilarated, she giggled. "I love to dance with you. And dinner sounds terrific. But I'd like to go home first and change."

"Good," he said, his face growing serious as she got up and finished dressing. "I'll pick you up in an hour."

She straightened her hair and wished she had brought something to freshen her makeup, but then she rebuked herself. She had never intended to make love to Chance Avery when she came over here today. She had reconciled herself to their not being meant for each other...and now...

Still, she couldn't help feeling a little ecstatic as he walked her to the door, kissed her one last time and stood watching her get into her van.

And as she drove away, she noticed the music was still playing. She hoped it would be for a very long time.

A BRASS ORCHESTRA played near the fountain at the Seven Seas, an exclusive seafood restaurant on the outskirts of town, where Chance felt sure no one would see them and report the news back to Jeanie.

He had been lucky to get reservations on such short notice, but he felt luck was with him tonight. Simone had dressed in a black crepe dress with crossed straps in the back, and as they followed the maître d' to their table, he couldn't keep his eyes, or his hand, from the bare spot on her back.

They sat near a tall window overlooking Lake Ford and saw the popular Hartford party boat drifting by, its lights cutting through the night. But it wasn't the sight of the lights on the lake or the Spanish moss dripping down from the trees just beneath their window or the music playing softly and serenely in another part of the restaurant that had Chance mesmerized.

It was the wondrous look in Simone's eyes, the pleasure on her face, the smile on her lips.

"I've never been here before," she said. "It's beautiful."

"I've never been here, either," Chance admitted. "It's the kind of place you have to share with just the right person. But I think it was worth the wait."

She caught his eyes and gazed into them, almost shyly, and he smiled at the blush scaling her cheeks. "I think so, too," she whispered.

He took her hand and leaned toward her, blocking out the waiters scampering by and the sounds of other diners nearby. "You really look beautiful tonight," he said.

She smiled. "Thank you." She covered her face and shook her head, and he saw her blush deepening. "Why do I feel like I'm in the middle of a fairy tale, and any minute you're going to turn into a frog or something?"

Chance chuckled softly. "I'm not saying it couldn't happen, but I can maintain a sense of charm when the need arises."

"Then it's an act?" she teased. "Something not to be taken seriously?"

His smile faded at the apprehension in her eyes. "No, it's no act. I'm not that smart. I leave all the tricks to my daughter."

"Then all this charm... Where does it come from?"

He pointed to his chest, in the region of his heart, and offered her a tender smile again. "Right here," he said.

The words couldn't have done more to fill the void in Simone's soul, and as the waiter approached their table to take their orders, she thought how she didn't ever want this moment to end. He was hers alone tonight, and she was his. Tomorrow was a million years away.

THREE HOURS LATER, when they realized they were the last couple in the restaurant and the orchestra had stopped playing for the evening, they went downstairs to the bar, where a three-piece band was playing "When a Man Loves a Woman."

Not yet ready to break the fairy-tale spell, Chance coaxed Simone onto the dance floor.

It was different this time, she thought, as she laid her head against his shoulder. The first time they had danced, they were in the spotlight, with hundreds of teenagers watching and Jeanie serenading them. The second time they had danced on dirt at dusk, with the band right on the other side of the door. Tonight they could have been the only two people in the world, for they had no awareness at all of anyone else around them.

The double glass doors of the bar opened onto a deck, where the breeze swept across the lake and cooled the room. Slowly, as the song droned on, Chance danced her through those doors and into the quiet stillness of the night. She looked up at him and saw that he was watching her, his eyes more serious than she had ever seen them. Their lips met in silent supplication, soft and sweet and heart-meldingly intense, and it suddenly occurred to her how dangerous this could be. She was feeling too close to a man who had the power to break her heart. She was investing emotional energy on which she might never get a return. She was allowing hope to blossom where it might never be allowed to grow.

Their kiss broke and he looked at her, his eyes glistening with the reflection of lake water and moonlight. "I think I might be falling in love with you, Simone Stevens," he whispered.

Tears welled in her eyes and she whispered, "Me, too, maybe."

He hugged her tightly, closely, almost desperately, and that, along with the sweet words she had wanted so badly to hear, illuminated the dark places of her heart where she had feared to tread for so long. She felt herself getting more familiar with those chambers of her soul that only Chance had been able to open, and she knew that if she ever let anyone into them again, it would be him.

CHANCE GOT HOME at one o'clock, still floating on air from the headiness of being with Simone. He couldn't believe he had told her he thought he loved her on their first real date, but then nothing about their relationship had progressed normally. The thing was, he had meant it. Every word. And her response, as timid as it was, had touched his heart in a way that it hadn't been touched in years.

Smiling, he went to his room and kicked off his shoes, and slipped his tie from around his neck. Wouldn't Jeanie be surprised if she knew they had gone out together, that he had fallen in love with her, that he couldn't stop thinking about her?

Slowly he sat down on the bed and told himself how dangerous it was to build up his daughter's fragile hopes about creating a "real" family again. He was right to keep quiet about his relationship. He was right not to let Jeanie know.

And yet he wanted to shout to the world that he was in love with a wonderful woman.

It was hard keeping quiet. It would get even harder, he suspected.

He took off his shirt and tie and went into the hall to check to make sure all the doors were properly locked. Jeanie's door was closed, and he told himself that was just one more sign that his daughter was growing up. For most of her life, she'd insisted on sleeping with the hall light blaring into the bedrooms, because she'd been afraid. Even now, she never closed the door and kept a Mickey Mouse night-light burning in her room. Had she stopped doing that without his noticing?

Something about that sudden change struck him, and silently he opened her door and looked in. He couldn't remember Jeanie ever sleeping in complete darkness like this. Especially when she was home alone. Usually, on the rare occasions when he'd come in late enough that she'd gone on to bed, she left every light on in the house.

A sudden burst of paternal love filtered through him at all the changes his baby was going through now. Before he knew it, she wouldn't be afraid of any of her childhood ghosts, wouldn't need her father at all. She would be off to college with a life all her own, and the house would be empty and dark all the time.

He went to her bed, leaned over and straightened her covers in the darkness.

And that was when he realized there was no one under them.

Flinging back the covers, he saw the pillows she had carefully lined up to look like herself.

"Jeanie!" he shouted. He went to the window, saw that it was slightly opened. Pulling it farther up, he shouted again, "Jeanie!"

He rushed outside, and saw that the band members' cars were all gone. Still, he ran to the barn and threw open the door. No one was there.

"Damn it!" he shouted, then ran back in, grabbed the telephone book and began dialing the numbers of her friends. If it was the last thing he did, he would find her. And it might turn out to be the last thing *she* did, as well.

Chapter Ten

The crowd at the Yankee Dime was bigger than Jeanie had expected, and as she and the other band members began tuning their instruments and checking sound levels, she felt a queasiness she hadn't had to deal with before. Brian worked on tuning his guitar with a look of doom on his face, and just before it was time for them to start playing, he pulled Jeanie aside.

"I don't like this one bit," he said. "I want you to know I'm gonna see to it that this never happens again."

Jeanie touched her nervous stomach and peered out at the partyers waiting for the music so they could burn off some of the booze they had already put away. It had never occurred to her that she would be in a place like this at sixteen, let alone performing here. And despite her need to wipe her guilt out of her mind, her promises and assurances to her father kept fleeting through her heart. "It's all right. I really don't want to hold the band back," she said, though the mist in her eyes belied her enthusiasm.

"The band will survive," Brian said. "You're the key to any success we've had, so you don't have to feel bad about saying no to anything."

"I do feel bad," she said. "I don't like feeling like a kid. And if I'm committed to the band—"

"You don't have to commit to playing in nightclubs, Jeanie. We'll do the best we can tonight, but I mean it. No more."

Jeanie sighed and went backstage, frustrated that the others couldn't understand her dilemma. No one but Brian seemed to care what this was costing her.

The stage lights came on and the band was introduced, and as she had done at the high school, Jeanie came out singing.

The crowd's applause set her immediately at ease, and she realized that she was "making it" in a club with people five to ten years older than she. If she could do that, she could make it anywhere. With or without her father's blessing.

As the applause began to intoxicate her, she lost all her inhibitions and threw heart and soul into her performance. And suddenly her worries about her father, her age and her relationships with the members of the band were far out of her mind. All that mattered was putting on the best show she could. All that mattered was proving that she was somebody.

THE PHONE RANG just as Simone was climbing into bed, and reaching across her pillow, she answered it. "Hello?"

"Simone, it's me, Chance. Jeanie's gone."

"Gone? What do you mean, gone? Did she run away?"

"No, I don't think so. She didn't take anything with her. But she's not here. She staged it to look like she was asleep in bed, but she's gone."

"But it's after one. Where could she be?"

"I don't know," he said. "Could you call Brian and see if he heard her talking about any plans she might have after practice? I'm really worried."

"Of course. I'll call him right now."

She hung up, and quickly dialed her parents' phone number. Her father answered in a groggy voice. "Hello?"

"Dad, I'm sorry to wake you, but I need to talk to Brian."

"Who is this?"

Simone gave a chagrined grunt. "I called you 'Dad.' Who do you think it is?"

"Simone?"

"Please, Dad, I need to speak to Brian."

She heard the rustling of sheets and him muttering something to her mother.

"Simone?" Her mother sounded as awake and spry as she always did, and Simone rolled her eyes.

"Yes, Mom, it's me. I need to speak to Brian."

"Well, he isn't home, honey. I don't know what to do about him. I mean, can you give a curfew to a boy of eighteen? *Should* you? I never had this problem with you, but then I don't suppose you had anywhere you wanted to go as badly—"

"Mom," she cut in. "Where is he? Did he say?"

"No. I thought he was at band practice, but he really shouldn't be making all that racket at this hour...."

"Mom, if he comes in, will you tell him to call me? Leave him a note on his pillow or something. It's really important."

"Of course, honey. Are you all right? I tried calling you tonight."

Simone sat on the edge of her bed and shoved her hair back out of her face. "Yes, Mom. I was out on a date."

"A date? With George?"

"No, not George."

"Taylor, then."

"No, Mom. Somebody new. I'll tell you about it later, but right now I have to find Brian."

"All right, dear," her mother said. "But if there's something about him that makes you not want to tell me about him, then I can only imagine the worst."

"Such as?"

"Well, maybe he's married. Or maybe he's a convict. Or maybe he's got some dreaded disease. . . ."

"Mom, it's one in the morning. Do we really have to do this now?"

When her mother only sighed, she realized that, yes, they did have to do it now.

"All right, Mom. He's the father of one of my students."

"Oh, my God. He *is* married."

"No, Mom. He's a widower. He's very nice and I'll tell you all about him later, but right now I have to go."

She got in a quick "goodbye" before her mother could work in another question, and hung up. Quickly she dialed Chance's number, but it was busy. Frustrated, she hung up the phone, turned on her light and sat on the bed waiting for him to call her back.

"THEY DID WHAT?" Chance clutched the phone as if he were throttling Jeanie's neck, and tried to listen better to Neal's roommate. He had already grilled the parents or answering machines of everyone else in the band.

"They had a gig, man. The Yankee Dime. It was sort of last-minute."

"The Yankee Dime? Are you telling me that my little girl is in a nightclub?"

"Hey, man, I don't know nothin' about nobody's little girl. But that's where Neal is."

Chance slammed down the phone and picked it up again, shaking as he started to dial Simone's number. When she answered, he practically hissed into the phone, "They're playing at the Yankee Dime!"

"What?" Simone asked. "I called Brian, but he wasn't home.... He... The Yankee Dime? Are you sure?"

"Positive," he said. "And I'm on my way over there right now."

"Chance!"

"What?"

"I want to go with you," she said. "Please... It won't take ten more minutes to come get me first. Will you do that?"

"What the hell?" he bit out. "You can keep me from killing somebody once I get there."

He slammed the phone down and bolted out the door, ready to do serious damage to the walking hormones who had dragged his daughter into a sleazy nightclub.

"IT'S ALL YOUR fault, you know."

Simone closed the car door behind her and gaped at the man sitting behind the wheel—the man who, just hours ago, had been a veritable Prince Charming. "*My* fault? How do you figure that?"

"If you hadn't talked her into being in this band, my daughter wouldn't be singing in some nightclub right now." He slammed the heel of his hand on the steering wheel and screeched out of her driveway.

Simone started to protest, but she couldn't find the proper defense for herself. She *had* encouraged Jeanie to be in the band.

"Damn it, I *told* you what would happen. That they would corrupt her. That she'd change. My daughter never lied to me in her life before all this. Now she shaves her head, sneaks out at night..."

"Chance, calm down," she said. "None of this is doing any good. I don't know what could have happened to make them do something like this. Brian promised me—"

"Brian promised you," he mocked. "Brian's eighteen years old. Do you honestly think an eighteen-year-old boy has any morals? Do you honestly think he cares about promises to his sister...or me for that matter?"

"He *does* have morals," she said. "I know my brother. There must be an explanation. When we get there, we'll hear it, and I'm sure—"

"When we get there, we won't have time to hear anything," Chance said. "When I get through with

Jeanie, I have a good mind to call the police and report the club for letting a minor on the premises."

Simone shot him a horrified look. "Chance, you can't. Please, just do this quietly. If you run in there and humiliate her in front of everyone, that will only make her more rebellious. Being defiant to declare her independence is bad enough, but being defiant out of anger is a lot worse."

"Forgive me if I don't listen to your brilliant philosophy this time," he snapped. "I let her be in the band, and she defied me. I didn't punish her for dying her hair blue, so she shaved it. She's told lies, she's sneaked out, she's broken my rules...."

"It all looks really bad right now, I know," Simone said, trying to calm her voice and hoping his would calm as well. "But Jeanie's a good kid. She doesn't mean to keep bucking your rules, but peer pressure is pretty overwhelming. It's a war zone for these kids."

"I'll show you a war zone," he bit out. "When I get there, they're going to think the atomic bomb just hit them. And my daughter will never forget it."

Simone cringed and decided to keep her mouth shut for the rest of the ride.

THE APPLAUSE SWELLED as Jeanie's best song came to an end, and she squinted through the lights and saw that the dance floor was still full, even though it was nearing closing time. The band launched into the next song, and she closed her eyes and belted out the first lyrics.

And then she opened her eyes and her gaze drifted over the crowd. It stopped at the door. A man had just come in, and he was glaring at the stage.

"CHANCE, NO!" Simone grabbed Chance's arm and tried to hold him back, but he jerked free. "Don't go up there. Wait until the song's over!"

"The hell I will," he said, working his way through the crowd. "She's not going to sing another note in this place if I have anything to say about it!"

"But there are better ways to do this than grabbing her down in front of everyone. Chance!"

Chance broke free of her, and Simone looked up to see that Jeanie had seen her father coming. She kept singing, while looking at him, as if hoping beyond hope that he'd be reasonable about this. But she should have known better.

Horrified, Simone watched as Chance stalked up the stairs to the stage, took the microphone out of his daughter's hand, and said, "Show's over, folks."

Then, grabbing his daughter's hand, he dragged her, fighting him all the way, off the stage and back through the crowd.

The audience began protesting loudly, and the band's music died a sudden death as the musicians gaped, disbelieving, at the scene playing out before them.

Chance didn't utter a word as he took Jeanie out the door and dragged her through the parking lot to the car.

"Daddy, how could you?" Jeanie screamed, hot tears of humiliation streaming down her face. "You ruined my life! How could you do that to me?"

Chance opened the back door to his car. "Get in."

"No! I won't! You've humiliated me, Daddy. I'll never be able to show my face again! In front of all those people, you treated me like a little kid."

"You acted like a little kid," he bit out. "Now get in the car or I'll put you in myself."

Sucking in a sob, Jeanie got in and only then noticed Simone. "Did you see what he did?"

"I saw," Simone said, slipping into the front passenger seat as Chance got in on the other side. She shot him a censuring look, but didn't say a word.

"Daddy, you've *ruined* me! It'll be all over school by morning, and nobody will ever ask us to play again...."

"You don't have to worry about that," he clipped, cranking the car and jerking it into reverse. "This was the last performance you'll ever have to worry about."

"Daddy! I know I shouldn't have gone without permission, but it was a last-minute opportunity. They were paying us and everything, and I couldn't hold the band back, and if I asked I knew you'd say no!"

"Damn right I would have."

"But, Daddy! I didn't plan this. I didn't deliberately set out to hurt you!"

"I've heard enough, Jeanie," he said through compressed lips. "I suggest you can it for a while, before I really lose my temper."

Knowing it was no idle threat, Jeanie fell silent, except for the sounds of her hiccuping sobs in the back seat, as they rode home.

When he turned down Simone's street, she looked over at him, searching her mind for something to say to settle his anger. But nothing came to her. He pulled the car roughly into her driveway and she opened the door.

"I'll . . . I'll see you later?"

He jerked the stick shift into park and looked over his shoulder. "Jeanie, stay here. I'll be right back."

Breathing a sigh of relief that he didn't plan to drop her out without resolving what had just happened between them, Simone got out of the car and followed him to the front door. She unlocked it and he stepped inside, his face as hard and emotionless as she had ever seen it.

"Chance, I'm sorry this all had to end this way. After the day we've spent together . . ."

"Look, this whole thing..." He threw up his hands and raked his fingers through his hair. "Damn it, this whole thing has been a mistake. I should have never listened to you about my daughter. What in the hell do you know about raising kids?"

"Chance, don't say something that you'll regret. I didn't tell Jeanie to go play in a nightclub."

"No, but you promised me she wouldn't."

"She has a mind of her own. I didn't know this would happen."

"But I did!" he shouted. "I did, and I listened to your instincts instead of my own. I let my own hormones dictate how I fathered my daughter!"

The words had the impact of a slap across the face, and she jumped back, glaring at him. "Hormones? Are you saying that's all it was? Just sex? All the sweet talk, and the affection, and the dancing . . . All it was was hormones?"

"No, that's not what I'm saying, but I wasn't thinking clearly. I let your screwed-up philosophy influence me, and that was stupid! I'm her father. You're just her teacher. That's all."

As if someone had dropped her heart from the top of the Empire State building, Simone felt it hit bottom. "I...I never assumed I could be anything more."

"Good," he said. "Because... maybe our first instincts about this relationship were right. Maybe it's not a good idea. Maybe I just need to concentrate on my daughter for a few more years. Maybe I don't have any business letting myself get so preoccupied with a woman that I'm not watching my daughter."

"So it all boils down to one or the other?" she asked, hating herself for the tears pushing into her eyes. "You couldn't have decided this before I slept with you? Before I believed you when you told me you loved me?"

As if he'd suddenly been doused with more weariness than he'd ever known, he slumped back against the door. "I'm sorry I let us get ahead of ourselves, Simone, but it's never too late to see our mistakes. The mistake would be pretending that we're right for each other, and going on."

"I see." She wiped a hot tear singing down her face, and opened the door for him. "Then... I'll see you around. At the hearing, I guess. I suppose you'll have plenty to tell them now."

He breathed a silent laugh. "I honestly don't know what I'll tell them, Simone."

Then, without another look back, he left her standing at the door and got back into his car.

Simone closed the door and held herself together as she heard the car pulling away. But the moment it was gone, her misery and self-deprecation and despair rushed in on her. She had known better than to fall in love with him. To believe he was different from any other man. She had known better than to make love to him. To believe the unuttered promise of something more... a relationship... a secret commitment...

And she knew better than to think she could get over him now.

The worst part was that Chance blamed her for every bad thing that had been happening in his life, and he was probably right. She had interfered. She had encouraged Jeanie to do something that her father didn't like. She had taken a liberal view based on no parental experience, just ideas that seemed like a good idea at the time.

In just a few days, Chance would hammer the final nail in her coffin, and now she questioned whether she should even fight it. Maybe all those parents were right about her. Maybe she was just screwing up a lot of vulnerable, young lives.

Too exhausted to talk herself out of those fatal charges, she collapsed on her bed, fully clothed, and cried herself to sleep.

JEANIE SLAMMED OUT of the car before Chance had even killed the engine, and stormed into the house. Chance was behind her in an instant.

"Turn around here to me, young lady! We have some talking to do!"

"I have nothing to say to you!" Jeanie screamed, her face raging red and her makeup smeared pathetically under her eyes. She ran to her room and slammed her door behind her.

"Jeanie, come back here! I'm not through talking to you!" Chance bellowed, but his protest fell on deaf ears, for Jeanie wasn't budging.

Furious, he went to the books he had on child rearing, the ones he referred to often, jerked one out of its bookcase and thumbed through the pages looking for the chapter on children who sneaked out of their homes to perform in nightclubs. But there wasn't one. What his eyes fell on, instead, was the chapter on "Discipline with Dignity." Cursing under his breath, he flung the book across the room.

There wasn't a book that told fathers how to do what was right for their daughters. There wasn't a book in the world that could tell him how to react properly when his little girl could be in jeopardy without even knowing it. There wasn't a book in print that could tell him how to smile his way through her adolescence, or keep her from growing up so fast, or make her understand that he only cared about her.

And neither Simone nor anyone could pass judgment on him for doing what he thought was right. Even if his daughter never spoke to him again.

Chapter Eleven

Simone couldn't even manage a "hello" when her brother showed up at her front door before she had even gotten dressed for school the next morning. "What do you want?"

"Sis, I know what you're thinking," he said, coming in without an invitation and closing the door behind him. Dino panted at his feet and began to whimper to be acknowledged. Still talking, Brian leaned down and scratched the dog's ear. "We were wrong to take Jeanie there, and I admit it. I should be shot for letting it happen."

"No," she said, walking into the kitchen and getting her piece of toast out of the toaster. It burned her hand, so she dropped it. Dino retrieved it and swallowed it in two gulps before she had the chance to pick it up. "First, Brian, you should be tortured. Slowly. And after days and days of endless agony, *then* you should be shot. I'd even pull the trigger myself."

"Okay, I deserve that," Brian said. "But it wasn't Jeanie's fault. Could you talk to her father and tell him that? I'm afraid of what might happen. He might make her get out of the band—"

"Might?" She flung around and gaped at him, astounded. "Brian, you can bank on him making her get out of the band. And that's the least of it. We're not talking about your stupid band here, Brian. We're talking about a young girl's self-esteem, and her relationship with her father—the most important person in her life."

"I know," he said, looking at her with a seriousness she hadn't suspected he was capable of. "I feel terrible about it. It all just got out of hand. I should have stopped it. But you can talk to him, can't you? You can fix it with him."

"Talk to him?" Simone laughed out loud, but there was no mirth in her voice. "Bri, Chance Avery has nothing to say to me. Except, of course, how I screwed up his daughter's life."

"You? What did you have to do with anything?"

"I'm the one who told him what a morally upstanding young man you were, and how you would never allow Jeanie to be compromised in any way. I'm the one who encouraged Jeanie to be in your band, and I'm the one who talked him into letting her stay in. But last night, you made me out to be an idiot, didn't you? An idiot and a liar."

Tears burst into her eyes, and Brian frowned and stepped closer. "Sis, I'm really sorry. I didn't expect you to be so upset by this."

"I am upset!" she cried, smearing a tear across her face. "Brian, what happened last night is going to have a serious domino effect. Besides affecting Chance's and Jeanie's lives, it affects mine. I could wind up losing my job over this. Chance is testifying at my hearing next week, and now I don't know what he's going to say. But I have a pretty darn good idea."

Brian leaned back against the counter, the helpless look on his face almost making Simone want to let up on him. But it was time he realized that every action had a consequence. *She* had finally learned.

"Wow," he whispered. "I did it again, didn't I? It's like I'm determined to get you fired."

She plopped down into her kitchen chair and dropped her face into her hand. He watched her sob for a few minutes, before he went to stoop in front of her, and tried to move her hand.

"Sis, are you all right?" His voice trembled with the question.

She looked up and drew in a long, deep sigh. "No, I'm not all right. I did something really stupid. Stupider than all the rest of this."

"Trusting me? That wasn't stupid. I let you down—"

"No, not trusting you," she corrected. "I'm talking about something else. I'm talking about falling in love. *Damn* it!"

"Falling in love?" Confused, Brian shook his head. "I don't understand." He stared at her, as if trying to figure out how this related to what they had been talking about before, when suddenly it dawned on him. "Jeanie's father? You're in love with Jeanie's father!"

Simone dropped her face into her hand again and began to cry harder. "So stupid," she said. "I knew it couldn't work out. It was doomed from the start, but I'm so stupid!"

"Hey," Brian whispered. "You're not stupid. Nobody ever chooses who they fall in love with. If it's meant to be, it'll work itself out."

"That's the point, Dr. Freud. It's not meant to be."

"Maybe not," Brian said.

She came to her feet, frustrated with his acknowledgment of the hopelessness of it all, but before she knew what had happened, he stood up and pulled her into his arms. As she wilted against him and wept into his shoulder, she realized that he had, sometime in the last year or so, grown taller than she. When had her baby brother become a man?

"You know, Simone, if Chance cares about you, he'll get over being mad. And if he doesn't, well... then he doesn't deserve you anyway."

She pulled back and wiped her face. "For a stupid idiot, you sure can be smart sometimes."

"I know," he said. "I just wish I could make you believe it."

"I do," she whispered weakly. She stepped back and managed a meek smile. "I really have to get ready for school. There'll probably be a lynch mob waiting outside."

"Sis?" Brian asked as she headed for her bedroom.

"Yeah?"

"I'm really, really sorry. If I could turn back time, it would all turn out differently."

"I know, Bri," she said, and crossing the room, she pressed a kiss on his cheek. "And I love you a lot. It'll be all right. Don't worry."

He nodded and watched, still feeling helpless, as she headed back for the bedroom.

CHANCE GOT UP extra early the next morning, which had been easy since he hadn't slept a wink. The things he had said to Simone last night—things he knew were hurtful but had been too angry to hold back—kept reeling through his mind like the lyrics to an off-key song. But it wasn't Simone he should be focusing on now, he told himself. Jeanie needed a parent who wasn't so preoccupied with life that he let her run wild. From now on, he would be a better father. And he would start with making sure she ate a balanced breakfast.

The smell of frying bacon, baking biscuits and scrambled eggs filled the kitchen, but Jeanie hadn't shown her face. Getting annoyed, he called back to her room. "Jeanie, you're gonna be late for school! Hurry up!"

He heard a door slam and then saw his daughter coming up the hall, her arms loaded with books. He didn't miss the look of absolute misery still on her face, and her eyes were swollen from crying. He doubted she had gotten a moment's sleep, either.

"You don't look so good," he said, his voice softening a degree. "Are you all right?"

"Fine."

"Okay." He scooped the eggs out of the pan and set them on her plate. "Breakfast is ready."

"I'm not hungry."

"Jeanie, you have to eat."

"If I do, I'll throw up."

From the look on her face, he didn't doubt her threat. "Jeanie, do you feel well enough to go to school today? It was a long night, and you could stay home—"

"I don't want to stay here with you." The words shot like a well-aimed spear through the center of his heart. "I have to go now."

He watched, unable to speak, as she gathered her purse and, still carrying her armload of books, headed out the door.

For the first time, it occurred to him that Jeanie could run away. Or worse, she could do something to hurt herself. His stomach knotted as he went to the window and watched as she pulled her little car out of the driveway. She had never looked quite as miserable as she had just now, and despite how angry he still was with her, the worry ate at his heart like the advanced stages of a disease.

He turned to the phone and wished to God that he could call Simone and spill his heart about Jeanie, but hers would be hardened to him after the things he had said last night. How could he make her understand that it wasn't just his heart at stake when he fell in love, but Jeanie's, too? How could he explain that he had to consider what was best for her, even if his heart told him differently? But the logic and rightness and self-sacrifice of his decision didn't help the emptiness gaping inside him. He hadn't expected to be hurting over her when the relationship had barely gotten off the ground. Why had he let his emotions get all tied up in knots, when he needed more than anything else to keep a clear head?

He had enough problems without thinking about her. After all, she *was* to some extent responsible for what had happened. But he was responsible, too. He couldn't deny that.

Again, he peered out the window, but his daughter was out of sight. His heart felt heavier than he remembered it feeling since his wife died, and the thought sent dread pulsing through him. He didn't want to feel that way again . . . not ever. And yet there wasn't a damn thing he could do about it.

Grief wasn't something you could put out like a fire. He had hurt before, and he knew the pain would have to run its course, for all of them. And sooner or later, Jeanie would get over the humiliation and misery he had inflicted on her, and he would stop being so angry at his daughter and so confused over Simone. Sooner or later, things would get back to normal.

But that normality didn't seem so appealing anymore, if Simone wouldn't be in the picture. Now "normal" seemed empty, lonely, dead.

But that was the way it would have to be, he supposed. Because fate had been against them from the start.

SIMONE DRAGGED THROUGH school that day, unable to generate any enthusiasm for the work she usually loved. It didn't help when Jeanie was the first of her third-period students to come in. Without saying a word, the girl slumped in, wilted and weary.

"Jeanie, are you all right?"

"No, I'm not all right," she said, avoiding Simone's eyes. "Would you be?"

"No, probably not." She went to the empty desk across from Jeanie, knocked a cape and wig off the seat and sat down. "Look, everything that happened last night was unfortunate. But that doesn't mean we can't still be friends."

"I don't need any friends," Jeanie said. "I don't need anyone."

"But, Jeanie—"

"My father made me get out of the band, okay? You can tell Brian for me. And the only reason I came to school today is that I couldn't stand the thought of staying home with my father. But it doesn't mean I have to like being here."

"Nobody said you did," Simone whispered. "Look, why don't you call Brian yourself?"

"No, I can't." Tears burst into her eyes, and her face twisted with the effort of holding them back. "I don't want to talk to him. I don't want to talk to anybody who saw what happened last night."

"Jeanie, Brian doesn't blame you. He blames himself. I talked to him this morning and he's really upset about everything that happened."

"He'll get over it," Jeanie said.

"But will you?"

For the first time that day, Jeanie looked Simone in the eye. "Probably not."

"Well, I hope you're wrong about that."

Two students ambled in and others followed. Not able to say anything else without being overheard, Simone started back to the front of her room. She sat quietly at her desk as the class filed in and waited for the bell to ring. Lacking the exuberance or the confidence to use her usual methods of teaching, she turned her lifeless face to her students. "Turn to Chapter Twenty-two in your books, please," she said.

The students gave each other strange looks, as if an impostor had just inhabited the body of their favorite teacher, and each moaned out his protest. But Simone barely heard. All that got through to her was the apathetic, downtrodden look on Jeanie's face, and the fact that her efforts to boost her up had done worse than failed. They just might have destroyed her entirely.

THE BAND'S VAN pulled up to the barn at four-thirty that afternoon, and Jeanie realized Simone had given Brian the message. She watched from her bedroom window as they opened the doors and began loading their equipment into it.

Tears ran down her face, and she collapsed back on her bed, staring at the ceiling. What were they thinking of her? That they should have known better than to recruit a kid to sing with them? That she had not only embarrassed herself, but them? That they were better off without her?

The doorbell rang, and she sat up and wiped her face quickly, and ran to the window to look out again. No extra cars were in the drive, and Chance was in the kennels. It had to be one of the band members, but she just couldn't make herself face him.

The bell rang again, three times in succession, and finally taking a quick glance in the mirror to straighten her hair and wipe away her tears, she went to answer it.

Brian stood before her, looking as awkward as she felt. His hands were crammed into the pockets of his jeans and he swallowed as he offered her a crooked smile. "Hi."

"Hi," she said. "I was in the middle of something—"

"Can we talk?" he cut in. "Just for a minute?"

She hesitated for a moment. "I'm not allowed to have boys in the house when my dad isn't here."

"Any rule against talking to them outside?" he asked.

"There probably would be, if he thought I was talking to one of you."

"It won't take a minute," he said, "and the last thing I want to do is get you in more trouble. But I really want to talk to you."

Shrugging, as if she didn't care one way or another, she stepped outside and closed the door behind her. She saw some of the guys coming out of the barn and quickly headed around the house. "I don't want to have to talk to them," she said quietly. "Let's go in the back."

Brian followed. "Why don't you want to see them?"

"Because," she said through her teeth. "I've never been so humiliated in my life. I want to crawl into a hole and die."

She reached the fence in the back yard, and leaned against it, looking away from him, but he didn't miss the tears filling her eyes. "Jeanie..." He reached out for her hand, but she recoiled.

"Look, Brian, there's really nothing to say. You don't have to be nice to me. You can just break down the equipment and take it home, and none of you has to give me another thought."

"I can't help giving you another thought," he said.

She looked at him then and their eyes locked for a long moment, as she searched for the meaning that hid behind his words. But there was no hope left in her heart.

"Jeanie, I'm so sorry for what happened last night. I'm sorry I didn't stop the guys from pressuring you and I'm sorry I didn't just flat out refuse to go to that gig. If I had, maybe it would have been easier for you. And I'm sorry that you're quitting the band, because the truth is that we've never had a better singer...ever. And I'm sorry your father hates me now, because I would really have liked to get to know you better...apart from the band. Now he'll probably never even let you around me again."

She stared at him, stricken, for a long moment, when suddenly a movement from the side of the house caught her attention. She saw her father standing there, holding a puppy in his hands, listening to everything they had said.

"Oh, great," she said, as her face turned a raging shade of red. "Now you're spying on me! Did you hear enough, Daddy?"

Before Chance could answer, Jeanie ran into the house and slammed the door behind her.

BRIAN STOOD AS FROZEN as Chance for a moment, staring at the door where Jeanie had gone. Then, feeling as if he had been caught at something again, he faced the man.

"Mr. Avery, I just wanted to talk to her for a minute...."

"I heard what you said." He set the puppy down, dusted off his hands and stepped toward the young man. "I wasn't eavesdropping. I didn't even know you two were back here. I just heard the last part."

Brian slid his hands back into his pockets and shrugged. "Well, I guess I'd better go help the band load all the equipment. We're sure gonna miss practicing here. It was a good place."

Chance didn't answer.

Brian started to walk away, but turned back. "Mr. Avery, I'm really sorry about all this. I can't tell you how sorry. None of it should have happened. . . ."

"I know," Chance said.

"You know, I really like Jeanie. I probably don't have any right to ask you, but I'd like to see her sometime. . . ."

"Do you mean date her?" Chance's words were too abrupt and harsh, and they took Brian slightly aback.

"Well...yes, sir. If you'd let me. I'd make sure I had her home by her curfew, and we'd tell you exactly where we were going." He looked at Chance as if trying to judge his expression, but it was too tight. "'Course that's probably out of the question, huh?"

Chance stooped down and caught the puppy as it started to scamper away. Absently he stroked its coat and looked at the door again. "I don't know," he said quietly. "It might be a possibility. You'd have to ask her."

"Really?" Brian's face brightened instantly. "I didn't think you'd want me around anymore. I mean—"

"I told you, I heard what you said to her. I'm not an unreasonable man, Brian. Despite what Jeanie thinks, I try to be fair. I'm not some kind of monster." His voice broke and he stood back up, completely focusing on the puppy, who scratched and squirmed to get down.

"Thanks, Mr. Avery."

Chance felt the ache of despair weighing heavily on his chest and he decided to go back to the kennel before he broke down completely in front of the boy.

"Tell her I'm going to call her, okay?"

"Maybe you'd better just do it," Chance said quietly. "You see, my daughter isn't speaking to me right now. She might not be for a very long time." He shrugged and tried to look less affected. "Call her tonight. I won't be home from about seven to eight, because I have to deliver this puppy to a family across town. If I'm not there, she might actually come out of her room to answer the phone. No visitors while she's alone, though."

With that, he walked away, leaving Brian standing alone in the yard.

IT WAS ALMOST dark when Simone's doorbell rang, and for the most fleeting of moments she thought that maybe it was Chance. Her heart flipped, then crashed, when she realized he would be the last person to knock on her door tonight.

She opened the door and saw Brian standing there, looking like someone who had lost his best friend, as well. "Can I come in?"

Simone let her brother in, and only then noticed that she had been sitting in a dark house.

"You have something against electricity?" he asked.

Simone shook her head and turned on a lamp. "I didn't realize it had gotten dark."

"Were you sleeping?"

"No. I was...thinking."

"Oh. Moping."

"Not moping," she argued. "I said thinking."

"Thinking about moping," he insisted. "But don't feel so bad. There's a lot of it going around. Where's Dino?"

"Out back working on a tunnel to the yard next door. One of their chihuahuas is in heat." Simone tossed a hand toward the kitchen. "Get yourself a drink, if you want one."

"No, I don't," he said. "I just wanted to come by and talk to you about Jeanie. I saw her this afternoon, and she's in real bad shape."

"I know," Simone said. "I saw her today, too."

Brian didn't sit down, but paced back and forth across the floor, thinking as he talked. "See, the thing that bothers me the most about her is that she's lost so much. I never expected for her to lose anything. It's not fair."

"You knew that if she got caught last night she'd have to leave the band," Simone said. "It shouldn't surprise you, and the truth is, it *is* fair. Chance had to do something. He can't just let her get away with sneaking around."

"I'm not talking about the band. I'm talking about what she's lost with her father. I think this has ruined their relationship, and it's the worst thing that could happen to her."

The thought of either one of them losing the other tightened Simone's heart. "She'll forgive him soon."

"I'm not so sure," Brian said. "You should have seen the way she looked at him today. I think she really hates his guts. It's killed something in her spirit, and I don't know what to do about it."

"Brian, there's nothing you can do."

"But I really like her," he said. "I want to help."

"Hey!" Simone frowned up at him, trying to sort out what he was saying. "Are you interested in her? I mean, apart from the band?"

A half grin tugged at Brian's lips. "Maybe...yeah, a little."

"Or a lot?" Simone asked.

"Maybe," he said again. "And Mr. Avery said I could take her out...."

"What?" Simone sat up straight in her chair. "He told you that you could take her out? Are you sure you understood him right?"

"Yes," Brian said.

Simone wilted back in her chair and frowned as she stared off into space. "I wonder why?"

Brian grunted. "Well, the answer is obvious. I'm a great guy. Who wouldn't want their daughter going out with me?"

"Maybe a man who had to drag her out of the nightclub you took her to last night?"

"Well, I redeemed myself, I guess. He overheard my apology to her, and I guess it was the first time he heard how it really happened. He doesn't seem to blame me that much."

"Amazing," Simone said. "I can't believe it."

"He has a mean temper," Brian said, "but he seems to get over things fast."

"Brian, why don't you talk to her? Try to make her see that he was only acting out of worry for her."

"I tried," he said. "I've been calling all afternoon, but she isn't answering the phone. I thought maybe you could help."

"Me? What could I do?"

"You could talk to her."

"But Bri, if she isn't answering the phone..."

"You could go over there tonight. Talk to her face-to-face."

Simone couldn't believe how ludicrous the suggestion was. "Chance isn't going to let me talk to her. He hates me!"

"He won't be home," Brian said. "He has to deliver a puppy to somebody, so he'll be gone around seven. Don't you see Sis, if I went over there, it would be like sneaking around or something. He tells me he's not gonna be home, so I show up right then? I don't want to get her into any more trouble. But there's nothing wrong with you going. Please, Sis, Jeanie needs help right now. She'll listen to you. I know she will."

Simone sighed. "Brian, talking to Jeanie and having her listen is what got us all into this in the first place. I have to learn to stay out of these things."

"But how can you? Don't you care about her? Think of poor Mr. Avery, moping around that place like he doesn't have a friend in the world. You'd be helping him, and if you really love him like you said you did..."

Simone closed her eyes, wishing she had never broken down and confessed her feelings to her brother. But she had, and he was going to use them against her now if he could. The sad fact was that he was right.

"All right, Bri. You've sold me. I can't bear the thought of Chance losing his daughter. It breaks my heart."

"Mine, too," Brian said, but his smile belied his words. "Call me the minute you get home."

"So you can make your move?"

Brian grinned. "The sooner we get her straightened out, the sooner I can get her to go out with me."

Simone couldn't help offering him a weak smile. "I don't think you'll have any problem doing that, Bri. Jeanie may have bad judgment sometimes, but she's no fool."

Chapter Twelve

Simone found Jeanie sitting in the dim yellow light of a single bulb in the loft of the barn, playing with three of the puppies that her father was selling that week. Quietly Simone climbed the ladder.

"Jeanie?"

Jeanie jumped slightly and looked up. "What are you doing here?"

"I came to talk to you."

"About what?"

The suspicious tone made Simone pause before leaving the ladder, as if she needed an invitation to come completely into the loft. "About your dad."

"He's not here," Jeanie said. "He had to deliver a puppy."

"I know. Brian told me. He's worried about you, you know."

"Brian? Why?"

As if Jeanie's hint of interest was the invitation she needed, Simone stepped off the ladder and knelt before the girl in the hay. "He cares about you, and he thinks this silent treatment you're giving your father is hurting you even more than him."

"It's not hurting me at all," Jeanie said. "I have nothing to say to him."

Simone drew in a deep sigh and let it out in a rush. "Jeanie, honey, this isn't like you. You're not yourself—"

"Neither are you," Jeanie cut in.

"Me? What do you mean?"

"I mean that you've fallen into the trap of being like all the other teachers. You're teaching from your book now, and everybody has to sit in their desks and take notes. Nothing like it used to be when we were actually learning something."

Simone wasn't quite sure how the subject had switched to her. While she didn't really want to discuss it, she couldn't ignore Jeanie's perspective, either. "I've been a little...disheartened lately. And a little cautious. This hearing next week, well, it could be the end of my career."

"But the reason you liked your career, the reason you were so good at it, was because you were different."

"Yes, well, sometimes I lose my confidence, you know?" She picked up a chubby puppy, stroked it until it squirmed, then set it down. It romped a few feet away and burrowed playfully into the hay. "Sometimes I'm not sure if I'm making a difference," she went on. "Sometimes I don't have the heart to keep on trying."

"I know about losing heart," Jeanie whispered. "But you do make a difference, Simone. You make a big difference. I wish we could show you how much."

"Thank you." She touched Jeanie's hand and her eyes began to mist over. "But I didn't come here to talk about me. I wanted to talk about you."

Jeanie shrugged and waved her off, and offered a crooked finger to one of the pups to gnaw on. "Simone, you saw what my father did to me," she said in a flat, lifeless voice. Tears broke free of her eyes and rolled down her face, and she got up and walked across the hay. When she turned around, her face was half lit, half shadowed as she faced her teacher, and the light of the bulb caught the tears glistening on her face. "Times like this, I really miss my mom."

Her voice broke, and she tried to swallow back her despair. But it wouldn't be hidden. "I didn't know her very well. Don't even remember her. I was so young when she died. But times like this...when he does something so unreasonable and so terrible, I really wish I had her here. She would *never* have done that to me. I know she wouldn't. And she wouldn't have made me get out of the band, because she sang, too, and she would have known how important it was. She would have known how good it made me feel about myself."

"Would she also have overlooked the fact that you defied your father, lied and sneaked?" Simone asked quietly.

Jeanie wiped her face and shook her head. "No. Probably not. But she would have been more fair. She would have tried to understand why I did it."

Simone pulled her knees to her chest and leaned back against the wall.

"Teenagers have good reasons for everything they do, Jeanie. But that doesn't mean everything they do is right. And parents have good reasons for what they do, too."

"But I didn't want to let the band down! I got all caught up in the excitement. . . ."

"And your father got caught up in fear for your safety."

"But what I did wasn't so bad!" Jeanie cried. "I didn't rob a bank or get pregnant or call him to bail me out of jail! I didn't do anything that would hurt anyone!"

"You hurt yourself, Jeanie. And more than anyone, you hurt your father. He trusted you, and you betrayed that trust."

"But I didn't destroy him, Simone! I didn't humiliate him and embarrass him. He did those things to me!"

Her words hung like lightning in the air, creating an electrical charge that Simone didn't know how to break down. "Maybe you did something worse, Jeanie. You took away the most important thing in the world to him. His little girl. And now you're locked inside yourself, refusing to talk to him. I think that loss is a lot worse to him than humiliation or embarrassment would be."

Jeanie kicked at the hay and slapped at her tears, and mouthed a silent curse.

Sensing Jeanie's raging frustration, Simone got up and crossed the room, and reached out to the child who looked so small and so confused and so alone. "Jeanie, I know you're hurting, but you don't need to do it alone," she whispered. "Because you're not alone. You have your father. Some of us don't have any choice, but you do."

Jeanie fell into her embrace and clung with all her heart as her tears played themselves out.

CHANCE RECOGNIZED Simone's van the moment he pulled into the drive, and his heart did a little flip in his chest. And then he told himself that he couldn't feel that way, for it was over between them. Things had been said, bridges had been burned.... Whatever fragile, precarious bond they had formed was severed the night of the nightclub incident—the same night he had told her he loved her.

He got out of the car and went into the house, but it was empty, so he left it and looked in the kennel, where the dogs barked up a frenzy to see him. But neither Jeanie nor Simone was there.

Frowning, he walked across the lawn to the barn, wondering if they had gone there. He opened the door and peered in, and saw that only a small light bulb in the loft was lit. Quietly he stepped in and closed the door behind him.

Above him, he heard the soft, deep, hiccuping sound of sobs and sniffs. And then he heard Simone's voice, soft and comforting, and as intimate as it had sounded when she had spoken in his ear.

"You know, Jeanie, it's not easy to be a single parent. I'm not a parent at all, and sometimes it's all I can do to just take care of Dino and me. But your father...he's raised you since you were a baby.... All alone. Every day, the most important thing on his mind was you. Every day, his whole world centered around making a good life for you, making all the right choices, making all the right decisions."

"He *doesn't* make all the right decisions," Jeanie blurted. "Sometimes his decisions are wrong."

"Maybe," Simone said.

She paused, and he strained to see into the loft, but they were too far back. Instead he waited quietly, listening.

"But he tries. He does a better job than most parents I've seen. I don't think you have any idea how lucky you are."

There was a moment of silence, and Chance's face softened as he looked up into the loft. He wondered if Jeanie was beginning to think kinder thoughts about him, or if Simone thought of their times together more than she did the accusations and anger.

"Despite what you may think, Jeanie, your father's sole mission in life is not to make you miserable. He loves you, and he wants to see you happy. You just have to work with him on that sometimes."

Jeanie didn't answer, and he could only imagine her sitting on the hay, breaking a straw into tiny pieces, pretending not to hear.

"You know," Simone went on, "your dad deserves a lot more than resentment and hostility for loving and protecting his daughter. And you deserve a lot more than alienation and withdrawal. You're two pretty terrific people, and I hate to see either one of you so sad and alone."

"There are worse things than being alone," Jeanie said.

"Yeah, maybe. But from where I sit, it just seems such a big waste. When you have someone to love you, why turn it away?"

Chance felt a lump growing in his throat, and he raked his hand through his hair and stepped closer to the ladder, wanting desperately to climb in and see the look on Simone's face and on Jeanie's as they talked.

"Your father loves you more than logic, Jeanie," Simone said quietly. "And if anyone ever loved me like that, I'd do whatever it took to make him feel that love coming back to him. No matter how furious he made me at times."

A moment of quiet followed and he heard Jeanie crying again, and slowly, quietly, he climbed up the ladder, just enough to see that Simone was holding his daughter, letting her weep against her shoulder. Something about that sight sent a poignant warmth flooding through him, and he realized he hadn't known a feeling like that since the first time he had seen his wife nursing Jeanie. It was a feeling of gratitude and shared love.... But in itself that feeling forced him to confront his own sense of loss. For by his own choice, he had turned Simone away.

Simone pulled Jeanie back, wiped her face with the backs of her delicate fingers and breathed a ragged sigh. "I have to go now, Jeanie. He'll be back soon and I really don't want to run into him here."

"Why not?" Jeanie asked. "Would that be so terrible?"

"It just wouldn't be a good idea," she said. "I've interfered in your life enough. I don't want him to think I'm doing it again."

"If you're so afraid of making him mad, why did you risk coming here in the first place? He could hurt you bad at the hearing. He could make everything sound so terrible—"

Simone looked down at the hay, clutched a handful in her fist and dropped it. "I didn't want to see either one of you go on hurting." She sighed and her voice cracked. "Jeanie, I care so much for your father...and you. He's such a good person. He deserves to be happy."

She cupped Jeanie's chin in her hand and made the girl look up at her with her red, glistening eyes. "Will you give him another chance, Jeanie? When he comes home tonight, will you talk to him?"

"I don't know if I can," Jeanie whispered.

"Do it for me," she said. "You keep asking what you can do to help me with this hearing. This is what you can do. If you don't, then I'll believe your father's right about my interfering. Because of my suggestion that you get into that band, you are completely alienated from him. That's a lot of guilt to hang on me, Jeanie. And if I can't at least get the two of you talking again, then I don't really deserve to be teaching anymore, anyway."

She got up, dusted off her pants and quickly Chance went back down the ladder and stepped into the shadows where she wouldn't see him when she came down. He heard Simone saying goodbye and Jeanie's quiet promise that she would talk to him when he got home. His eyes filled with tears as he watched Simone climb down the ladder and leave in the darkness. For a moment, he struggled between going after her and staying to talk to Jeanie. He wondered what Simone would do if he ran after her and pulled her into his arms, and told her he hadn't meant it when he had ended things with her. But before he had sorted out his whirling emotions enough to move, he heard her van leaving the ranch. Defeated, he wiped his eyes and went back to the door, opened it as if he were just coming in, and called, "Jeanie?"

His daughter looked down from the loft, her eyes raw and swollen and still wet from her tears. "Daddy?"

Chance walked closer, staring up at her, his heart about to burst with the need to hold her and make everything all right. "Are you okay?"

"Yes." She burst into tears again, and quickly Chance climbed the stairs. When he reached the top, his daughter fell into his arms and clung to him with all her might.

"I'm sorry, Daddy. I'm so sorry I lied to you and I'm sorry I let you down—"

"I'm sorry, too," he whispered. "I never meant to hurt you...."

They both wept, wrapped in each other's arms, until Jeanie was able to talk again. "Simone was here," she whispered. "She came to talk to me about us. She made me see some things..."

He thought of pretending that he didn't know, but didn't have the energy for deception. "I know," he whispered. "I came in while she was here. I heard some of it."

Jeanie looked up at him. "Really? Why didn't you say something?"

"It seemed private," he said. "I thought maybe you just needed a woman to talk to."

Jeanie stared at him for a long moment and he waited for her to accuse him of eavesdropping, which was exactly what he had done. There was no excuse for it, and yet he hadn't been able to help himself.

"She's in love with you," Jeanie said, jolting his heart. "You know that, don't you?"

"No. I think it's you she loves."

"Maybe she loves both of us."

Shaken that his little girl could get to the heart of things so suddenly, he wondered if this were another ploy on her part to get them together. "Jeanie, I know you have visions of Simone miraculously becoming the mother you need, but things don't always work out the way you want them to, honey. Sometimes, things just aren't meant to be."

"I didn't want her for me, Daddy," Jeanie whispered. "You see, you've been alone all these years, and you deserve to fall in love." She looked up at him, with a smile that reached her eyes and even in the shadows illuminated all the love she felt for him. "I want her for you, Daddy."

Chapter Thirteen

Simone sat at her desk, as she had for the last twenty minutes, staring at the stack of papers that needed to be graded. But her heart wasn't in her work. Fresh tears filled her eyes—eyes already red and swollen from a sleepless night—and she dropped her face in her hands and asked herself how she would get through the day.

There were so many regrets lurking in her subconscious, so many yearnings, so many dashed hopes and dead dreams. And tomorrow, even her career was likely to be over.

The sound of footsteps coming up the hall made her quickly wipe away the evidence of her tears. It was still way too early for any of the teachers to report for work, but she supposed that there were others like her who saw no point in sitting alone at home.

But it wasn't a teacher she saw when the footsteps reached her classroom.

"Chance! What are you doing here?"

Heaving a deep sigh, he came in. "I wanted to talk to you before school started. I went by your house, but you'd already gone."

She raked a hand through her hair, suddenly sorry she hadn't taken more pains with her appearance. He looked as bedraggled as she, however, and she realized she had never seen him look so tired, or so tousled, or so troubled. And yet, at the same time, he looked more wonderful than she had ever seen him, for her heart was so starved for his presence.

"About what?"

"About what you did last night. Talking to Jeanie."

Hopeless defeat washed over her, and she closed her eyes and raised her hands to stem the inevitable confrontation. "Chance, I know you're probably mad at me for interfering again, but—" Her voice broke off and she stopped, desperately trying to hold off her tears.

"Simone, no." He crossed the room in three steps and leaned over her desk. "I didn't come here to blame you, but to thank you."

Simone caught her breath and looked up at him. Her tears still hovered in her eyes, blurring her vision. "Really? She's talking to you now?"

"Yes," he whispered. "Whatever you said, it got through to her. I really appreciate it. You made a big difference."

"Oh, I hope so." Her tears escaped over her lashes and streamed down her face, and suddenly she felt completely exhausted and without control. She dropped her face into her hands and her shoulders shook with the force of the emotion washing over her.

Without a word, Chance took her wrist, pulled her hand away from her face and pulled her to her feet. He slipped his arms around her and crushed her against him, and she grabbed his shirt in her fist and wept against him, angry at herself for being so fragile. She had to pull herself together, she thought. She had to get a grip on her emotions, before he realized just how torn up she was.

"Why are you crying?" he asked, his voice a deep rumble against her ear.

"Because... I'm so tired," she said. "Because... everything's so messed up. But... I'm glad Jeanie listened. One never knows."

"You're not supposed to know." He cupped her chin up to him and forced her to meet his eyes. His were misty as he beheld her. "You care, and that's what matters. The outcome is out of your control."

"Is it?" she asked, not convinced. Moreover, she wasn't convinced that he believed it himself. "The outcome is what keeps getting me into trouble."

"Maybe that's because of people with bad tempers who fly off the handle before they examine all the facts. People who pretend they don't feel the emotions they feel, just because it's so hard to reconcile them with everything else going on."

She wouldn't allow herself to assume he was apologizing, or that he spoke of feelings he still held. She wouldn't allow herself to hope as she looked up into his eyes. For there was still Jeanie, and his feelings about her influence over her, and the hearing....

As if he read her thoughts, he whispered, "I'm sorry for all the things I've said, Simone. I'm sorry for blaming you for Jeanie's normal adolescent behavior. I'm sorry for blaming you for her defiance. And I'm sorry for blaming you for trusting her as much as I did."

He wiped the tears from her cheek, and she tried to keep her heart from running away with the possibility that he wanted to resume things. He had apologized, yes, but that didn't mean he wanted her.

"She's a good kid," Simone said. "She really is. She's going to sow a wild oat or two, but she's been brought up really well and she's not going to stray too far."

She saw the emotion shadowing his eyes, and he said, "Yeah. As long as she doesn't get as screwed up as her old man, I guess she'll be all right."

"You're not screwed up," she whispered. "You know exactly what you want. And you know what you don't want. There's nothing wrong with that."

He framed her face with both hands and gazed down at her. "Simone, that's not the case at all. I've been so confused.... So lonely. I've been thinking about you night and day...."

She closed her eyes, and knew the pain in her face was there for him to see, in all its humiliating glory. For confusion and desire weren't enough. He had made up his mind that they weren't good for each other, and who was she to argue with that?

"About the hearing tomorrow..." he said.

She held up a hand to stop his words and slipped out of his arms. Unable to face him when he said what she didn't want to hear, she turned away, pretending to sort papers on her desk. "Just tell them the truth, Chance. That's all I could ask of you."

"I plan to." She felt him watching her, waiting, and she closed her eyes and tried to stop the new tears from squeezing out.

Gently he laid his hands on her shoulders and turned her back around to face him. Again, the sight of her tears made his own eyes glisten and he swallowed hard.

"The truth," he whispered, "is that this school system can't afford to lose a woman like you. And maybe I can't either."

Stricken, she gaped up at him. "What?"

"That's what I'm going to tell them," he said. "Not the part about me, but I'm going to tell them how valuable you are to the county, and how they can't afford to let you go."

"Really?"

"Really."

A smile broke through her tears, and she slid her arms around his neck and hugged him with all the strength her fatigue would allow.

"I miss you, Simone," he whispered, and before she knew what had happened, he was kissing her, the way he had that first time, when her heart had melted into her bloodstream and she had felt herself falling too fast to save herself. With him, there were no safety nets, there never could be. But once again, she found herself willing to take the risk.

"Excuse me!"

They jumped apart and broke the embrace, and looked at the doorway, where Edith Seal, the school-board member who lived across from Simone, stood watching them with disgust and rage in her eyes.

"I was just delivering a memo from the school board," the woman said, still holding her lips as tight as rubber bands, "but I had no idea I'd be interrupting such an intimate little scene."

Simone wiped her eyes and gave Chance a helpless look. "We were just...talking...about his daughter."

"Yes, I can see that," the woman said. "You do realize, don't you, that the students will be coming any minute now? I'd hardly think that's a very good example for them when they get here. But then it wouldn't be that far removed from anything else they see in this class, I don't suppose. Tell me, Miss Stevens. Have you shared your stripper with your students, yet?"

Simone snatched the memo out of the woman's hands. "Thank you for delivering the memo, Mrs. Seal. Now I'm sure you have things to do, don't you?"

"We all do," the woman said, "what with the hearing tomorrow and all. It should be very interesting."

The woman pranced out and Simone turned back to Chance, her face as red as her eyes.

"I'm sorry, Simone," he whispered. "I've done it again, haven't I?"

"You haven't done anything," she whispered, staring down at the memo. "It's just inevitable, that's all."

Chance glanced over her shoulder and saw that it gave the time and place of the hearing, and outlined how it would be conducted. "Simone, I swear, I'm going to do my best to help you tomorrow."

"Thank you," she said without much heart. "I appreciate that."

The flat, dull tone in her voice deflated his heart, and he glanced out and saw that students were beginning to fill the hallway. "Well, I'd better let you get to work."

"Yeah."

"I'll see you tomorrow."

She nodded, but couldn't make herself say more as he blended into the students milling through the corridor.

THE DOORBELL RANG just moments after Jeanie came home that afternoon, and she opened it to see Brian standing there with his guitar.

"I thought I'd come by and see how you were doing," he said. "I've sort of missed you since you quit the band."

The bold admission hit her squarely in the heart, but she told herself not to let it show. Still not allowed to have a boy in the house when her father wasn't there, Jeanie stepped outside and pulled the door closed behind her. Jamming her hands into the pockets of her jeans, she said, "I've missed you guys, too."

The fact that she included the others didn't seem to escape him, for his face fell slightly. He went to the porch swing, sat down and set his guitar in his lap. After a moment, Jeanie sat down next to him.

He started strumming, and she recognized the tune as "Michael Row Your Boat Ashore." Unconsciously, she started humming.

He started to put more emotion into his playing as she hummed, and when he started singing the words, she smiled and began to sing, too. Her voice drifted sweet and melodious over the ranch, complementing the wind and the whispering of leaves.

When the song was over, she laughed aloud. "I haven't sung that song since I was a little girl at camp."

"It was beautiful," he said. "Darn, I love your voice."

Again, her smile faded, and she looked into the breeze, trying not to dwell on her disappointment at having to let her talent go to waste.

"You shouldn't stop using it, you know," he said, as if he could read her thoughts. "You should join the choir next year at school, or start singing at church, or *something*..."

A smile inched across her lips again. "You think so? I hadn't really considered that."

"Your father would be happier, and you'd still get to show off your talent."

She looked out over the grounds and considered the possibility. "Yeah, maybe."

"Either that, or I could just start coming over every day and play for you," he teased.

She grinned. "That might not be so bad."

"Really?" Brian took the guitar off his lap and set it down, and leaned it against the house. Shifting, he faced her. "You mean you wouldn't get all tired of me and start thinking of ways to get rid of me if I came over more?"

She giggled quietly. "Of course not."

He breathed out a sigh of relief and flopped back on the swing. "Oh, thank goodness. After getting your father's permission to ask you out, I would have felt like a real jerk if you'd told me to get lost."

His rambling hit the core of her realization, and she frowned. "You really talked to my father?"

Suddenly, Brian's face fell serious, and he took her hand and laced his fingers through hers. "Jeanie, I'd really like to take you out sometime, if you want. I mean, if you don't, just say so, but I was kind of hoping—"

"I'd love to go out with you," she blurted, then chastised herself for not keeping cool.

He smiled. "Really? Oh, good." He let out a breath of relief, then laughed off his tension. "Uh . . . well, how about tonight? No, it's a school night. Not good."

She couldn't help giggling. "How about tomorrow night? It's Friday."

"No, tomorrow's bad," he said. "My mother is planning this big family meal in case Simone loses her job. How about Saturday? Where do you want to go?"

"I don't care."

"Neither do I," he said. "Maybe I'll just surprise you."

She bit her smile and told herself that squealing with excitement might come across as just a bit immature. "Sounds great."

He picked the guitar back up, strummed it again, and breathed a laugh. "Now that that's out of the way, do you know 'Sittin' on the Dock of the Bay?'"

CHANCE SAT, half-reclining, in his chair, and stared at the blank television screen.

He thought of Simone, and how ragged she had looked today. She hadn't been sleeping, and tonight would probably be the toughest night of all for her. Tomorrow could be a turning point in her life, and there was nothing she could do to stop it.

He started to phone her, then hung up. A call wasn't likely to help, he thought. Maybe she needed company. Maybe tonight she needed a friend.

Pulling out of his chair, he went to the door of Jeanie's bedroom. "Jeanie?" he whispered.

Still awake, Jeanie sat up. "Uh-huh?"

"I'm going out for a little while," he said. "Will you be all right alone?"

"Of course," she said, indignant. "I'm not a baby."

"I'll lock the door behind me. Don't answer it for anyone."

"Daddy, I'll be fine," she said, lying back down.

He looked at her for a moment, his heart swelling with love for the girl who had meant so much to him over the years. But she was right; she wasn't a little girl anymore. And somehow, her love wasn't enough for him. He needed someone else.

He needed Simone.

He drove to her house, not certain what he would do or say when he got there. But somehow, it didn't matter. Tonight, all he wanted was to hold and comfort her and, if he could, in some small way help her get through the night.

SIMONE SAT NEXT to Dino on her couch, her school diaries for the last three years spread out on the cushions next to her. She had spent hours combing through them day by day, looking for clues as to who would be testifying against her tomorrow, and trying desperately to jog her memory about crucial—and perhaps fatal—conversations she had had with her students.

But nothing was very clear, for her notes were very cryptic and not detailed. And they didn't capture the essence of the student's pain, or her own desire to help, or the outcome sometimes months later.

Weary to her soul, she laid her head back on the sofa and tried to relax so that she could sleep. But sleep had eluded her for the past few days, and she feared she might never find it again.

A knock sounded on the door, and she jumped and got to her feet. It was eleven o'clock, and she wasn't expecting anyone. And here she was dressed in her robe, with bare feet peeking out, her hair as disheveled as if she had just rolled out of bed, and her face as bare of makeup as it had been on the day she was born.

Apprehensively she padded to the door and tried to see through the peephole, but it was too dark to make out who her visitor was.

"Who is it?" she asked quietly.

"It's me. Chance."

Her heart jolted, and quickly she opened the door. He stood before her like a phantom in the moonlight, his eyes glistening with apprehension and emotion that reached across the threshold and grabbed hold of her heart. "Chance? What are you doing here so late?"

"Did I wake you?" he asked.

"No. I couldn't sleep. Come in." She stepped back to let him in, but only then caught sight of Mrs. Seal walking her dog across the street. "Oh, Lord. Mrs. Seal saw you come in here."

"What does that woman do, anyway?" he asked, looking back over his shoulder. "Police the whole area day and night?"

"No. Just me."

He hesitated in the doorway, then shook his head. "Look, I'll just leave. I didn't come here to get you into more trouble."

"No, please stay!" she said, and suddenly realized she had been too emphatic. It wasn't good to give that much of herself away. Tempering her voice, she said, "To Mrs. Seal, my breathing causes trouble. I'm such a harlot, you know. She'd slap a scarlet letter on my chest if she could. In fact, that's probably one of her proposals to the school board."

Chance's smile was weak, but still he didn't come entirely in. "Still, there's no need to feed her imagination the night before the hearing."

"She's going to imagine no matter what you do," Simone said, and suddenly tears burst into her eyes, and her lips began to tremble. "Tonight I really need a friend, Chance, and I can't tell you how glad I am to see you. Please don't leave yet."

He came in and closed the door behind him, and decided that Mrs. Seal could be damned for all he cared. If Simone needed him, he wouldn't let anyone stand in his way of being here. "Come here," he whispered.

She fell willingly into his arms, and realized it was the first time since that morning—the last time he had held her—that she had felt at peace. Nothing seemed so threatening when Chance was holding her. Nothing seemed so hopeless.

He led her to the couch and pulled her down across him. Cradling her in his arms, he whispered, "I couldn't sleep, knowing what you must be going through."

"I'm all right now," she said. "Just hold me for a while."

She laid her head on his shoulder as the tears played themselves out. After a moment, she looked up at him. "I'm getting your shirt all wet."

He smiled and wiped her face with gentle fingertips. "That's what it's there for," he said. He reached down and kissed her, so soft and sweet and undemanding, that she felt her spirit coming back to life, stretching and preparing itself for tomorrow's fight.

When the kiss broke again, he wiped the tears from her face and laid her head back on his shoulder. "Close your eyes," he whispered. "Try to sleep. I'll stay and hold you for a while."

As if the words were all the tranquilizer she needed, she felt herself relaxing into him. In the deep rumble of a voice that she loved so much, he began to hum the tune to an old folk song that she barely recognized and couldn't name. The sound coaxed her under layer after layer of sleep, and as the song wound on, she stopped thinking and worrying and feeling.

Wrapped safely in the cocoon of Chance's arms, she fell sound asleep.

Chance, too, dozed for a while, but he woke around midnight and saw that Simone was engaged in a deep, restful sleep, still wrapped safely in his arms. Gently he lifted her, carried her to her bed and tucked her under her covers.

She didn't wake as he sat next to her on the bed, watching her sleep and wishing from his soul that he could crawl in next to her and be there when she woke up. But he had Jeanie at home, and she needed him, too.

For the first time, it occurred to him how lonely it would be, waking in his own bed alone tomorrow. For the first time, he admitted how nice it would be if Simone were an everyday part of his life. For the first time, he realized how deeply involved with her his heart had become. Too involved to turn back, he thought. Too involved to save himself now.

He bent over and pressed a soft kiss on her temple, feeling the sleep warmth of her face, and pushed her hair back from her eyes. She was beautiful, he thought, and not in the same way that Jeanie was beautiful. She was sensuality and sexuality, security and belonging. She was every good feeling he had ever known packaged into one. She was love in a unique form...a form he hadn't really known in fourteen years. The kind of love that gnawed at your soul if you denied it, but that flourished and blossomed if you fed it.

And that, he vowed, was what he intended to do.

Quietly, he slipped out her front door, and locked it behind him.

The woman across the street was gone and all her lights were turned off. Careful not to slam his door, he got into his car and drove home.

And despite the events that would draw them together tomorrow, he couldn't wait to see Simone again.

Chapter Fourteen

Chance couldn't believe the number of Simone's accusers waiting to be called into the hearing the next afternoon. Their chairs were lined against the walls in a square, like those in a therapy group, and the fervor in their conversations about Simone worried him more than anything else he had considered so far.

Their tongues wagged in whispers and muffled voices, while each "witness" went in one at a time, and each time the door opened Chance strained to see Simone's face. She sat at the table with the school board, and she looked even more drawn and strained than she had the night before.

At least he knew she had gotten some sleep.

The other accusers, at least ten of them, sat calmly as they rehearsed lambasting Simone to each other. He regarded the woman across from him, who looked as though she had had lemons for breakfast and hadn't yet gotten the sour taste out of her mouth. "And now Katie's pregnant," she was saying, "and it's all that woman's fault."

He felt his hackles rising, and even though the words weren't addressed to him, he cleared his throat and interrupted. "Excuse me. Did you just say it's Simone's fault that your daughter got pregnant?"

"Not *my* daughter!" the woman exclaimed. "Mrs. Allen's daughter. The one who's in there right now."

Chance's face tightened. "Are you telling me that she blames Simone because her daughter is pregnant?"

"She sure does," the woman said. "And so do I."

Chance couldn't help the bitter laughter rising up inside him. "I could have sworn that it took a man and a woman to make a baby. How in the world could that have been her fault?"

"She told Katie where she could get birth-control pills, that's how."

Chance frowned. "But I thought you just said the girl was pregnant."

"She is."

"Well, if she had taken the pills, she wouldn't be, would she?"

"She *didn't* take them," the woman said, waving him off as if he couldn't grasp what she was saying. "The point is that she all but gave the girl permission to have sex. Made it seem all right, as long as she was protected."

"Well, it sounds to me like the girl was already having sex, or they wouldn't have been having that conversation in the first place. And if the girl had listened, maybe she wouldn't be in this mess."

"That teacher had no right to discuss sex with Katie in the first place!" the woman bit out. "Just like she had no right to talk my son out of going to Georgia Tech!"

Chance's frown grew more pronounced. "You're here because of that?"

"Yes!" the woman said. "I went to Georgia Tech, my husband went to Georgia Tech, and all of our children are going to Georgia Tech. She talked Sammy into applying for admission to some out-of-state college, despite how adamantly he knew we felt about it, and even showed him how to get his out-of-state tuition waived. There's been nothing but trouble in our house ever since!"

"Heaven forbid," Chance said, slapping his face sardonically. "I say they not only fire her, but hang her up by her toenails and shoot spears into her!"

"My point is that she *influences* those kids! She has too much power over them."

"Maybe that's because they respect her."

"Maybe that's because they worship her. Like a cult leader or something."

Heat flushed his face, and he turned to the only man in the room, the man who had sat there quietly fidgeting since he had come in.

"What about you? What are you going to tell them?"

The man braced his elbows on his knees and studied his palms. "If you don't mind, it's rather personal. I don't care to discuss it outside of that room."

Chance shrugged. "All right, if you say so."

The door opened, and the witness who had been inside came out, smiling as if she had accomplished some great feat. The principal looked at his clipboard and said, "Mr. Latham? It's your turn."

Chance caught a glimpse of Simone again as the man ambled into the gym, and his heart sank another level as he read the doomed expression on her face.

SIMONE RACKED HER BRAIN for the complaint the man sitting before her had made against her, but for the life of her she couldn't remember. Had Mr. McCall deliberately not mentioned it to her?

She sat back, holding her breath, as the man told his name and the name of his son. Vaguely she remembered the boy being in her class at the first of the year, but for some reason she had never been told, he had been transferred out within the first month.

"Mr. Latham, would you please tell us a little about the complaint you filed against Miss Stevens?" Mr. McCall asked.

The man gave her an embarrassed half glance, then focused on the school-board members instead. "You have to understand," he told them, "that I am a pastor. I expect a lot from my children, and I can't allow anything sinful or perverted to enter my home."

Simone frowned and looked at the school-board members next to her, trying to anticipate what was coming. Perverted? Sinful?

"I have never had any trouble with my son before. Never. He's been a perfect child. He's sixteen, and he's never had a drop of alcohol, no trouble with drugs, and he really doesn't even date that much. Spends a lot of time at church functions..."

"Uh...Mr. Latham, if we could get to the problem."

"Well...he had been in her class a couple of weeks, when I found some things he'd been hiding under his bed."

"What kind of things?" Simone asked aloud, even though she had been warned not to speak. The principal shot her a stern look, but she drilled her eyes into the man.

"Pictures. Of you."

"So?" Simone asked.

"Miss Stevens, you've been asked to keep your comments to yourself. I'll ask the questions."

Simone sighed and sat back in her chair, waiting for the man to go on.

"My son had...pictures of *her*...naked."

"What?" Simone came to her feet and glared at the man. "That's impossible!"

"Let him go on!" the principal shouted. "Miss Stevens, I'm telling you for the last time to sit down."

Simone wilted into her seat as tears burst into her eyes.

The man took a deep breath, as if the effort of going on took too much from him. "Well, they weren't pictures of her...exactly. He had cut her head out of some of her pictures...snapshots he had taken, pictures in last year's yearbook...and had glued them onto some *Playboy* pinups. Where he got those magazines I'll never know, but there she was, her head glued to those naked bodies...."

Simone dropped her face into her hands as a feeling of utmost defeat washed over her. Couldn't these people see how ludicrous this was?

Deciding that she couldn't just sit here and say nothing, she tried again. "Mr. McCall, this is ridiculous. I had nothing to do with his fantasies, or with his buying *Playboy* magazine. I didn't even give him the pictures!"

"He'd never *had* a fantasy like that until he was in your class!" the man blurted.

"He'd never been sixteen before, either," she retorted. "He's probably having fantasies about all sorts of women, not just me. That's what sixteen-year-old boys do. I didn't do anything to perpetuate that."

"Miss Stevens, that'll be enough." The principal stood up and shook the pastor's hand. "Thank you for coming in, Mr. Latham. We realize it wasn't easy for you."

Simone looked around at the stony faces of the board members. That they hadn't laughed the man out of the room frightened her more than she wanted to admit.

At the end of the table, she saw Mrs. Seal staring at her with smug eyes, as if she had finally gotten her where she wanted her. And she knew that it was just a matter of time before they told her to pack her things and leave the premises. All that was left to do was wait.

AS THE AFTERNOON dragged on, Chance became more and more tense, for he realized that things weren't looking good for Simone. Each time the door opened, she looked a little more beaten, and the witnesses coming out looked a little prouder of themselves, as if they had just been big contributors to curing cancer or spreading world peace.

Finally he was the last one sitting in the hall waiting to be called in, and he realized they had saved him for last for a reason. Because he had changed sides, he wasn't going to be taken seriously.

The door opened and he stood up as the last witness came out, and the principal nodded for him to come in.

Chance went into the gym and looked at the weary faces of the school-board members, who were obviously ready to wrap the whole thing up and go home. Simone looked worn out and absolutely crushed as he took his seat. Her eyes were red and her lips trembled, as if she would burst into tears now at any moment.

"Mr. Avery, it's been a long day," the principal said, "and we've heard plenty. If you could make this short—"

"I'll get my say like everybody else did," Chance said.

"Yes, of course." The principal looked at Chance's file, scanned it and said, "If you don't mind my summing things up for the board, you've accused Miss Stevens of encouraging your daughter to shave her head, dye her hair blue and get into a rock-and-roll band. Am I correct?"

"Not really." Chance gave Simone a guilty look, but she averted her eyes. "The fact is, I was wrong about her telling Jeanie to shave her head. I think it's a matter of record that I revoked that complaint. Simone...I mean, Miss Stevens had nothing to do with that. As for the dye, that was a temporary spray that washed out that very night. And the band...well, she was trying to cultivate Jeanie's talent."

"Is your daughter still in that band, Mr. Avery?" the principal asked, and from his tone, Chance knew he had heard the rumors about what had happened in the nightclub. He wanted Chance to incriminate Simone further by rehashing it all right now, but he was determined not to.

"No, not anymore," Chance said.

"Would you care to tell us why?"

His chest tightened, and he looked at Simone again, but she still wouldn't meet his eyes. "My daughter is going through a rather rebellious stage," he said. "She's trying to declare her independence. I've had a few problems with her, but none of those have anything to do with Miss Stevens. My daughter is going to test her wings regardless of who's teaching her history. The fact is, her grade-point average has gone up overall since she's been in Miss Stevens's class, because she's beginning to enjoy learning more. And for the first time in her life, she's making *A*s in history. Miss Stevens has encouraged her self-esteem, and has made a marked difference—"

"Excuse me!" It was Mrs. Seal who interrupted, and all eyes turned to the woman. "I had to interrupt all this nonsense, because this man's testimony isn't the least bit credible. He, himself, filed a complaint against Miss Stevens, just as a dozen others did. Somehow, she managed to change his mind, and I don't think we should be subjected to this. It's common knowledge that he's having an affair with Miss Stevens."

Chance sprang out of his chair, almost knocking it over, and Simone dropped her face into her hands again. "She doesn't know what she's talking about!" he shouted.

"Oh?" the woman asked, smiling suddenly, as if she had elicited exactly the reaction she hoped for. "Are you going to deny that I saw you two clenched in a passionate embrace in her classroom yesterday, right in the open where any student could have walked in on you?"

Chance caught his breath. "There was no need to hide in the closet, since we weren't *doing* anything wrong!"

"One man's idea of right is another man's wrong," she said. "As you can see, ladies and gentlemen, he did not deny it. Neither will he deny that he spent the night at her house just last night."

"What!" Both Simone and Chance spoke simultaneously, and the woman's smile grew even more satisfied.

"That's right," Mrs. Seal said. "Tell me that I didn't see him coming to your house after ten last night, and that you didn't answer the door in your robe? Tell the board that the house wasn't completely dark and that he didn't stay there all night?"

"He did *not* stay there all night!" Simone cried. "He came over to see if I was all right, because he knew how nervous I was about today!"

"I left just after midnight," Chance said, then feeling more frustrated and angry than he had ever felt before, shook his head. "But wait a minute! What difference does it make whether I'm seeing her romantically or not? We're two single, consenting adults, and nothing we do has any bearing on whether or not Simone should be teaching here."

"Her moral standards have a great deal to do with her competence as a teacher," Mrs. Seal railed. "A woman who would entertain a stripper in her home shouting, 'Take it off!' has no business teaching teenagers."

Simone shot to her feet, and for an instant Chance feared she would bolt over the table and clench her fingers around the woman's throat. "I was *not* entertaining that stripper, Mrs. Seal. He was obviously entertaining *me!* And you know full well that I had nothing to do with his being there. My little brother—who I'll be the first to tell you has a warped sense of humor—sent him. And I'd dare say that if he'd been sent to strip for you it would implicate you just as much!"

"What is it with you people?" Chance's outburst drew the attention of the board members back to him, and he glared at them each in turn. "Are you all just out to crucify a decent teacher, or are you here to make an intelligent decision for the welfare of the students?"

"I think you know the answer to that," Mr. McCall answered, his chagrin apparent in the way he groped for the Rolaids in his coat pocket.

"Good," Chance said. "Then could we dispense with these ridiculous personal attacks based on rumor and overactive imaginations, and concentrate on the facts?''

''The fact,'' Mrs. Seal cut in, ''is that your lust for her has a great deal to say about your credibility.''

Chance felt a headache coming on, and if there was anything in life he hated, it was a headache. It made him mean, he thought, and sometimes illogical. And it shortened his patience to an unbearable level. He rubbed his temples and closed his eyes, and told himself not to let Mrs. Seal push him over the edge. Focusing his cold eyes on her, he said quietly, ''Whether or not I lust for Simone Stevens or even you, Mrs. Seal, has nothing at all to do with this hearing! *I'm* not on the chopping block here.''

He wasn't sure, but he thought he saw the beginning of a grin edging across Simone's mouth as the other board members gaped at him. Suddenly his head felt better.

Now that he had the board's attention, he sat back down and leaned forward, bracing his elbows on his knees, trying to meet the eyes of everyone at the table as he spoke.

''Now, if we could get back to the facts... It must be obvious to those of you who are sane—'' he shot Mrs. Seal a look that exempted her ''—that these allegations against her are ridiculous. Surely there isn't enough here to fire her.''

''It isn't just those allegations, Mr. Avery,'' the principal cut in wearily. ''It's also the fact that other teachers have accused her classes of being chaotic parties. I've seen it myself.''

"All right," Chance said, finally feeling as if he had something to work with. "Then test her students. See how they're doing in her classes."

"She has a higher quota of *A*s in her classes than any other teacher in the school, all right. That only means she's easy, not that the kids are learning anything."

"But couldn't it mean that she's teaching them in a way they understand?" he asked. "Couldn't it mean that she's getting through to them, and later when she tests them, they make *A*s because they remember what she's said?"

"It's possible," the principal said doubtfully.

"Then test them according to your standards," Chance suggested. "Give them the hardest test you can come up with for their age group, and see how they do. See what they know, and what they remember. See if she's teaching them anything."

For a moment everyone at the table was silent, then slowly, one by one, they began to nod and whisper among themselves. He met Simone's eyes, and saw the hope seeping back into them.

Mrs. Seal, however, wasn't going to sit still for anything that might help Simone's case. "It's a waste of time, Mr. McCall. All the other allegations..."

"All of the other allegations are very weak," the principal admitted wearily. "Mr. Avery is right. If we wanted to dig into the number of troubled kids in each class, we'd find the same types of stories. I'm not convinced that Miss Stevens is the cause of all these things."

"Another thing," Chance said. "This county has a huge dropout rate. Check the statistics. See how many students who have been in Simone's class at any time during high school really wind up dropping out. I'll bet you'll find a lot more kids staying in school than the average."

The principal frowned, as if he hadn't thought of taking such an approach, but finally he nodded. "All right, Mr. Avery. We're going to take your challenge. Monday morning we'll test her students, and I'll look into the statistics you suggested. Right now, I'm completely undecided about what action to take, and I think most of the other board members are, as well. I'd like to see the results of the test before I make a decision. Is that satisfactory to everyone?"

Mrs. Seal sat rigid as all the other board members voiced their approval. Simone looked at Chance, and in her eyes he saw the reluctant beginnings of joy, and the overpowering relief that it wasn't over for her yet.

"Then this hearing is adjourned until the results are in," he said. "I'll contact each of you Monday."

The board members stood up, stretching and gathering their papers, and Chance shot across the gym floor to where Simone still sat.

"I can't believe it," she said, gaping up at him. "They're really going to do it. You talked them into it."

"It's gonna be all right now. You'll see. They'll find just what we hope."

"Maybe," she said. "They have to. But even so, they could still decide I'm a bad influence."

"No, they couldn't be that narrow-minded."

"Believe me. They could."

The last of the board members filed out of the room, and he saw tears coming to her eyes again. "Hey, don't cry now, when I can't hold you without getting us both into trouble."

She smiled and wiped her eyes. "I think I could use a drink."

"Let's go, then. I'll follow you home and take you to get something to eat, if it's all right. Jeanie's spending the night with a friend, so I don't have to rush home. We can just relax and try to put this out of our minds."

She wiped her eyes and heaved a shaky cleansing breath. "I was supposed to have dinner with my folks, but I'm just really not up to it. I'll call and cancel," she said. "Let's get out of here."

Knowing that no one was watching, he took her hand and brought it to his lips. Pressing a soft, lingering kiss on it, he whispered, "It'll be all right, Simone. I know it will."

"It's going to be a long weekend."

"I'll be here to help you through it." More than any other reassurance he had given her that day, that promise told her that, indeed, everything would be all right.

"WHAT'S WRONG with me?"

The question came out of a gentle quiet that had followed them through their dinner at the restaurant and now dwelt within Chance's car as he pulled into his driveway. But it was a question that had hung in her heart all night, and she couldn't help uttering it.

"What do you mean?"

"I mean... all those enemies... all those people trying to do me in.... It couldn't be a coincidence that they all think I'm not qualified to teach." Her voice broke off, and she turned her face away and looked out the window. How could he understand what today had done to crush her self-esteem and her own confidence in her effectiveness as a teacher?

Chance pulled his car to a stop and cut off the engine, but he made no move to get out. "It isn't you," he said quietly. "Not at all. It's them. A bunch of people who fed off each other. One person blamed all the ills of her family on you, and someone hears about it, so they blame their problems on you, too."

If only it were so simple, she thought, but it wasn't. Today had been like a murder trial, with witnesses lined up to take their shots at her. "That's not it," she said. "You blamed yours on me, too. You weren't feeding off anyone."

"I was feeding off my own insecurities as a parent," he said. "I think we've both learned from it."

"Yeah," she whispered. "I sure have."

For a moment they sat silent in the car, contemplating the night falling over the ranch and the pall falling over their hearts. Finally he took her hand. "Come on. Let's go in."

The house was dark and quiet and Simone looked around, noting how warm and inviting it looked, even though Jeanie's shoes were lying in the middle of the floor where she had tossed them and Chance's newspaper was scattered beside his favorite chair. A pair of glasses that she assumed he used for reading sat on the table beside that chair and an empty glass sat on the coffee table.

It was a home, she thought, a home where everything was settled, where people depended on each other and knew that no matter how badly they ever screwed up, they wouldn't lose each other. A home where they knew their future and their past and they were familiar with each other. A home where they could take off their masks and be themselves, and no one would condemn or lecture or judge.

A home like she had always wanted. But living alone was safe, she supposed, because when she took off her mask there were no risks involved.

"Sit down," he said, taking her hand and pulling her onto the couch with him.

She sat down, curling one leg beneath her, and braced her arm on the back of the couch.

Chance touched her wrist with a fingertip, and ran it up and down her arm. "Simone, what I told the board members today was absolutely right. I'm having trouble with Jeanie because she's going through puberty, not because she's in your class. I want you to stop beating yourself up."

"Chance, you were absolutely right blaming me. I went too far when I found Jeanie a band and urged her to get into it before she got your permission. I was wrong to do that."

"But you were doing what you thought was right."

"But it was wrong, anyway. Don't you realize, that's what all those people were saying today? That my judgment is impaired? That when I do what I think is right, it turns out all wrong?" Her eyes filled with tears, and she covered them with her hand. "Maybe they're right. Maybe I shouldn't be teaching. Maybe I'm all wrong for it. . . ."

"Simone." He cupped her chin and moved her hand, and forced her to look up at him. "Listen to me. If there's anything wrong with you, it's that you're young and beautiful and single. People don't like young, beautiful, single women. It threatens them. They don't trust them."

Her tears flowed faster, and he smeared them across her cheek with his thumb. "Simone, when they test them Monday, everyone will see that you're not some frivolous little Pied Piper who's trying to put her students under hypnotic spells. They'll see that you're more competent than most of the teachers in the school, and that your students will suffer educationally if they let you go."

She sniffed back her tears and swallowed the lump of emotion in her throat. "Do you think so?" she whispered.

He pressed a soft kiss on her lips and nodded. "I know so."

Her eyes locked into his, and she saw the gentleness and sensuality that had radiated from him since the day they had met, when he had come to her classroom to tell her off. But he didn't condemn her anymore. Now he supported her.

Her eyes closed as he met her lips again, and she parted them as his tongue made a sweet, bold entrance. He stroked her tongue, then caught hold and suckled, tickling, teasing, exciting.

His arms pulled her tighter against him, hugging her with more force than passion could boast, for it went deeper. How much deeper, she was afraid to wonder, but she returned it with all her strength.

When he released her, his eyes were misty, serious, pensive, as he stroked her hair and kissed her forehead, her eyelids, her temples.

When he spoke, his voice was hoarse, shaky. "I love you, Simone."

She looked up at him, stricken. "Last time you said you *thought* you loved me."

"But now I know I do. I love you."

Tears burst into her eyes again. "But—"

He touched his fingertips to her lips to quiet her, and whispered again, "I love you."

She wanted to return it, to shout out that she loved him, too, but it was all so new, so frightening, and she felt like a porcelain doll taking flight off the side of a cliff. There was no place to fall but down, and when she hit she would be shattered.

As if he sensed her apprehension, he framed her face with his hands, and looking into her eyes said again, "I love you, Simone, and I know that's hard for you to believe after some of the things I've said and done. It's even hard for me to believe. But it's true, and I don't want to keep it a secret anymore."

"It doesn't seem to be a secret, anyway," she said. "Not after Mrs. Seal's accusations today."

"It's still a secret from Jeanie," he said. "I don't want it to be anymore. I don't want to sneak around with you. I want everyone to know how I feel about you. Especially her."

"But what if it doesn't work out, Chance? She'll be hurt, and—"

"No, Simone. If it doesn't work out, I'll be the one who's hurt. But I'm willing to take that risk, because I think we're on to something pretty damn good here."

A lump of emotions as big as her heart blocked her against him again. It was too sweet, she thought, feeling him hold her as if he could never bear to let her go. Feeling him love her with all the force within his soul. Feeling him cherish her as if she were someone to be valued. For the moment, she let herself believe in forever. For a moment, she let herself believe in the power of love.

"Oh, Chance," she whispered, knowing she took the biggest risk of her life by saying it, "I love you, too."

He caught her lips with his again, and this time his kiss was hot and wet and reached as deep as her core. Excitement exploded within her as he slid his hands over her, and suddenly they were both groping for zippers, fumbling with buttons, peeling layers of clothing away.

Bare flesh against bare flesh accelerated the rise of their desire, and getting to his feet Chance swept her up into his arms and carried her quickly to his bedroom.

There was no control, no censure, no presence of mind, as they explored each other and ministered to one another in ways that made heated memories and restless dreams. And when he joined with her, her mind and body detonated into a million jagged fragments. Together, they followed that fulmination with other eruptions, until she felt all those fragments coming back together, falling back into place. But the reassembling of her soul was different, somehow, for now she knew that they had intermingled their spirits in such a way, that separating now would take life-giving breath from each of them.

There was no turning back, and yet she wasn't entirely sure she could go further. There was too much darkness in her life right now, too much uncertainty, too much potential for heartache.

She looked up at him, touched his face and pressed a kiss on his chin. "Hold me, Chance," she whispered. "Help me to not be so afraid."

Chance didn't ask what she was afraid of, and she thought he probably knew. She was afraid of the school board and of losing her job. But more importantly she was afraid of who she would be afterward and who Chance would see in her. She was afraid of watching him fall out of love, as so many others had done, and she was afraid of wanting. For wanting always led to hurt.

"I'm not going anywhere," he whispered. "Just wipe the fears out of your mind. We can't solve all your problems tonight, Simone, but we can lie here and love each other. That's enough for now."

His words bathed her in a sweet wash of warmth and intimacy, and she knew this was the closest matching of souls she would ever experience in her life. And as she lay still beside him, entangled in his love, she decided that there was nothing else on earth that really mattered tonight.

THEY SPENT THE REST of the weekend together, though Chance was forced to leave her at her door on Saturday night, since Jeanie was going to be home at eleven from her date with Brian. But he was back at Simone's house the first thing Sunday morning, and when he told her his plans for the day she gaped at him in disbelief.

"You want to take me back to your place? With Jeanie there?"

"I told you last night that I wanted us to stop the secrecy," he said, stroking her freshly washed hair, and dipping his fingers through the still-damp curls. "Besides, I need to stay close to home. Spooner, my German Shepherd, looked like she might have her puppies today. I need to be there in case she does."

"Look, Chance, if you're too busy to see me to-day, you're really not obligated to count down the time with me. I have a lot to do here at home...."

"Simone," he said, cutting in and setting a quiet-ing finger on her lips. "I want to be with you today. I want you right there with me, and it has nothing to do with obligation. I'm counting down, too, and I'd rather we did it together."

She breathed out a sigh, and looked up at him. "Puppies, huh? Well, I guess that's one good way to get my mind off things."

"Guaranteed to pass the time and help put things in perspective," he said.

She smiled a weak smile, but didn't quite feel it in her heart. For Simone wasn't sure at all that she wanted things put in perspective. She wasn't ready for that kind of reality yet.

THE BARN DOOR creaked as Chance opened it and looked inside, seeking out Spooner who lay in the corner where he had left her that morning. "It's just me, Spooner," he said in a soft voice as he pulled Simone in behind him. "And I brought a friend. We're gonna keep you company for a while."

He heard a welcome whimper from the corner and saw Spooner huddled on her side, her breath short and shallow as she endured the last hours before birth. He went toward her and sat down on the hay next to her and moved his fingertips to scratch the back of the dog's ear. "Spooner, I'd like you to meet Simone. Simone, this is one of my best friends in the world."

Simone held out a hand for Spooner to sniff, then stroked her rich coat as she knelt beside her. "Is it all right for me to be here?"

"Sure," he said. "We'll just keep our voices low. Spooner's been a mom before, so this is nothing new to her. All we can do is wait."

"Well, I guess I'm getting good at that," Simone said.

"Yeah. Me, too."

The door opened, spilling in a triangle of light, and they saw Jeanie coming in. "Dad? I saw your car and didn't know where you were." She squinted through the dim light, as if she wasn't sure she saw clearly. "Simone?"

"Yeah, it's me," Simone said, shooting Chance a look that said he could still make up some story about why she was here if he wanted.

But Chance only grinned. "Simone's going to spend the day with us," he said. "Is that all right with you?"

"Well . . . yeah," Jeanie said. She walked toward them, looked down at Spooner, then at Simone and back to her father. "You two aren't . . . I mean you're not like . . . seeing each other, are you?"

"She's here, isn't she?" her father teased.

"I know, but she's been here before, and that didn't mean . . ."

"That we were an item?" Chance provided.

"Well . . . yeah." She turned her confused, but delighted, eyes to Simone, and asked, "Are you, Simone?"

"We've sort of been seeing each other a little," Simone offered weakly.

"Why didn't you tell me!"

"Because we didn't want you getting carried away with it," Chance said. "So don't."

She held up her hand in a mock vow, and shook her head. "I won't. I promise. It's just . . . such a nice surprise."

"And you didn't have to scheme or connive or manipulate anything to make it happen, did you?" Chance asked.

Jeanie gave a little shrug. "I don't know. I might have had a little something to do with it."

With that, she turned and pranced toward the door. "I'll leave you two alone now. Don't want to stand in the way of true love."

The door closed behind her, and Simone shot Chance a look. He began to laugh, and reaching across the dog, he gave her a long, lingering kiss.

Spooner whimpered between them.

"Sorry, Spooner," Chance said, "but it's like Jeanie said. You can't stand in the way of true love."

He kissed her again, then patted the hay next to him and she moved around beside him. Leaning her head against his shoulder, she petted Spooner quietly for a while.

She wasn't sure what made her ask, but suddenly it was important that she knew all the deepest scars in Chance's life. Suddenly she felt she had to know all his pain.

"Tell me about your wife," she whispered. "How did she die?"

He looked down at her, surprised at the question, but then he laid his head back over hers and answered. "A car accident," he whispered. "Why?"

"I just wondered. Was it terrible for you?"

She heard him swallow, and he leaned his head back against the wall and gazed up at the ceiling. "Yeah, it was pretty terrible. I loved her. I still love her. But time has a way of healing."

"Was she a good mother?" Simone asked.

Chance smiled. "Yeah, the best." He glanced over at Spooner, stroked her coat again. "I remember the day she went into labor with Jeanie. It was raining outside and she knew she didn't have long, but she didn't want to go to the hospital until she had to. So we played cards all afternoon, and along about five o'clock her water broke. And then all hell broke loose." He laughed aloud, then caught himself and lowered his voice for Spooner.

"You remember that episode on 'I Love Lucy' when Lucy goes into labor? It was about that crazy. But we got her there in time, and everything was fine."

"And only two years later she died?"

His smile faded and he kissed the top of her head. "Yeah. It was a real shock. I think for a while I was kind of angry about the whole thing. I wasn't that good of a father back then. I pretty much left it all to her. And then, wham, I'm left with this toddler all of a sudden. It seemed so unfair."

"But you did a wonderful job, Chance."

"Yeah, I did, didn't I?" he said with a wry grin. "Well, maybe not always. But I rose to the occasion. It's easy to do when you don't have any choice."

Quiet settled over them again as they both stared out into the hay at their feet, seeing replays of scenes in their past. Finally it was Chance's turn to ask.

"Why haven't you ever married, Simone? I know there must have been men who asked. A woman like you must have been in love before."

"I was," she said. "I was even engaged once. Almost went through with it."

"What changed your mind?"

"I didn't. He did. He decided I wasn't the kind of woman he could grow old with. I guess he got tired of trying to change me and decided at the last minute to pull out."

Chance frowned and cupped her chin to make her look up at him. "What in the world did he want to change about you?"

"Some of the same things you'd probably like to change," she said, meeting his eyes directly. "My flightiness, my spontaneity, the way I have of looking at things...."

"Wait a minute." He let go of her and shifted to face her, his eyes as serious as she had ever seen them. "Simone, there is nothing about you that I want to change. And if I ever gave you that impression, I shouldn't have. I love you *because* you're unique, and spontaneous, and because deep down—" he tapped her chest in the vicinity of her heart "—you have one of the best hearts I've ever known. You care about people, and I think that's the nicest thing about you."

"It gets me into trouble, though. Sometimes I think it's a good thing I'm only a teacher and not somebody's mother, because I could screw up some lives pretty good if I had a consistent influence on them."

"Simone, listen to me. I wouldn't have just let Jeanie in on what we've got going here if I thought that. You can influence Jeanie any time you want. I might not always agree with you, and I'll have the last word, but I'm not afraid at all of her talking to you. I've seen you with her, and I've heard the things you say. I have nothing but faith in you."

Tears filled her eyes, and she whispered, "Thank you, Chance."

"That's not all," he said. "That stupid thing I said that night, about your not being mother material. I never meant that. It was just one of those things you say to keep yourself from looking stupid. The truth, Simone, is that if I were to ever have another child, I would hope I could have it with someone as good as you."

One lone tear escaped her eye and traveled down her cheek as she stared up at him, absorbing the words that meant so much to her, words she had never expected anyone to say to her. Slowly she reached up to kiss him.

Their kiss was slow, sweet, lingering and loving, and in it she found security and comfort and peace from all the fears still haunting her. In it she found hope, and as if she finally had the strength to hold on to it, she reached out and took hold of it.

Spooner whimpered and tried to sit up, and Chance broke the kiss and turned around. "Uh-oh. Here comes number one."

Simone caught her breath. "You mean...she's having her puppies? Now?"

"Don't get too excited," he whispered, stroking the dog's coat and trying to keep her calm. "This could take a while. But it'll be all right, won't it, girl?"

Simone wiped the tear from her face and held her breath as she saw the first puppy crowning.

SHE DIDN'T GET MUCH sleep that night, for Spooner had six puppies, and she couldn't tear herself away from them for hours after they were born. Even then she could hardly relax, knowing that her students were being tested early that morning. Tense and tired didn't even begin to describe her when, late that afternoon, she entered the gym to face the board members again.

Simone studied their faces in turn, trying hard to tell which way they were leaning. Had her students let her down that morning? Had they remembered any of what she had taught them? Or had they been too distracted with dates and ball games to waste the time on a test they weren't even getting a grade on?

Mr. McCall was the last to enter the gym, and taking his seat, he dropped a stack of papers in front of him. Once he was settled in his chair, he passed the papers down the table. "I took the liberty of compiling all the test scores," he said, "and I'd like for each of you to have a copy."

Simone sat rigid. "Mr. McCall, could I have a copy, too?"

"Certainly," he said, and handed her one across the table. Before she had the chance to make sense of the scores, he took off his glasses, rubbed the bridge of his nose, then steepled his fingers in front of his face. "As you'll all see by these results, Miss Stevens's students scored well above average for their grade levels. In fact, the results were astonishing. We had obscure references in there to things that, I daresay, many of the teachers on this panel might have missed, and over seventy percent of her students answered the questions correctly. They indicated a keen understanding of historical events, dates and all, and were even able to express why those events happened and what might have prevented them. It was very, very impressive."

Simone breathed a gigantic sigh of relief and uttered a silent prayer of thanks for her students' putting forth the effort. If she didn't lose her job, maybe they *would* have a party. At her house, on a Saturday...if Mr. McCall would allow it.

"We also did the research Mr. Avery suggested, and found that of the students who take Miss Stevens's class, only eight percent have gone on to drop out of high school later. I don't need to remind any of you here that that's well below the county average of fifty-two percent." He stopped and cleared his throat, tapped his fingers together, and went on. "Whether that is a result of Miss Stevens's class is a matter we may never know, but if we can assume that she was responsible for all of the allegations we heard Friday, then we should at least give her credit for the good that comes out of her classes, as well."

It was as if a light was dawning in a dark and lonely tunnel, and Simone felt a smile seeping back into her eyes. She wanted to throw her arms around Mr. McCall and kiss him, but something told her that was premature. His face was still too guarded, and the other board members were not yet convinced.

Mrs. Seal stood up and faced the members of the school board...and Simone's hopes crashed. "If I may say something, Mr. McCall, I don't feel those tests are enough. Here she is, bopping around like one of her students, sleeping with their fathers, giving advice on their sex lives, leading them down the paths of destruction and wickedness.... She has to be stopped. We can't ignore the facts."

The principal shoved his glasses back on and picked up the report. "The facts you refer to are very circumstantial, Mrs. Seal," he said. "As a matter of fact, the *only* concrete facts we have are in these test results. Those others are all things that we could have pointed out in our classes when you were teaching, but no one ever suggested that you were responsible for them."

"I never counseled my students," she said. "I never told them to call me by my first name. I never made friends with them, as if I was one of them. No one could have ever blamed me for anything that happened to them."

"Maybe that's why so many of your students lost interest," Simone said, despite her vow to keep quiet. "Maybe that's why so many of them dropped out, and can't even get jobs at fast-food places now."

She waited for a gasp from the other board members, but oddly enough no one told her to sit down and be quiet. Seizing the moment, whether their silence was due to shock or agreement, she went on. "Mrs. Seal, I know you don't like me, and I'm sorry for that. But I care a great deal about each of my students. I've spent the last ten years of my life trying to find some way to reach them, and I think I've found it. It's my job to teach them history and that's what I'm doing, but I can't stop caring about them as people, too."

Silence filled the room, and Mrs. Seal turned to the principal, her face reddening, and said, "Mr. McCall, if this board elects to keep Miss Stevens on the faculty, I shall have no choice but to turn in my resignation as a school-board member immediately. I can no longer sit on a board that has such little regard for morals and values."

Mr. McCall cleared his throat again, shuffled the papers in front of him, and said, "We'll keep that in mind as we vote, Mrs. Seal. Now, if we could get on with it..."

Mrs. Seal gasped and turned her shocked eyes to the others in the room. "Did you hear what he said?"

"I believe they did, Mrs. Seal," the principal cut in. "Now, if you'll sit down so we can bring this matter to a vote. Miss Stevens, would you mind stepping outside, please?"

"Of course." Struggling with the surprise of Mrs. Seal's hidden ace—and Mr. McCall's reaction to it—she went to the door, and told herself that it wasn't over yet. Mrs. Seal might have sympathizers on the board, and this new development could only serve to make things worse.

Chance was waiting for her in the hallway, and the moment the door closed behind her he took her hand. "What happened?"

"They're voting. I don't know..."

"You're pale," he said. "Are you all right?"

Her lips trembled and she didn't know whether she would laugh or cry at what had just happened. "Mrs. Seal threatened to resign if they keep me. Mr. McCall didn't balk, but I don't know how it'll affect the others. They could all still take great pleasure in firing me."

He sat down next to her and set his hand on her shoulder, but she was as rigid and cold as stone. "It won't be long before we know for sure, Simone. And then it'll all be over."

She looked up at him, and suddenly an overwhelming fear washed over her. She didn't want him to be here when they told her. She didn't want him to witness the fall of her career, the collapse of her life, the destruction of her spirit. Making the decision even as she spoke, she said, "I don't want you to stay, Chance. I need to be alone for this."

He looked at her as if he had been walloped in the stomach. "But Simone, I can't leave you—"

"Please, Chance. If I could run away right now and go bury myself in those puppies and forget all this mess, I would. But if I have to stay, I want to do it alone. Go home and wait for me there. I'll come straight to your house as soon as I know."

For a moment he gaped at her, but finally he took the key. "All right. If it's what you want."

"I do."

With the greatest effort he'd had to summon in years, Chance gave her what she wanted.

She watched as he ambled up the hall and out of the school, then leaned back in her chair and closed her eyes. Failure wasn't something she'd had to confront often in her life, she thought, and she wasn't going to accept it gracefully. She didn't know how she might react—whether she would burst into tears like a sniveling idiot, or lash out at them in raging fury....

She prayed she would hold on to her dignity, but what if they told her it was all over? That she could never teach again?

Could she really go out to Chance's ranch and face him with it? She would have to, for she had promised. But it wouldn't be easy.

The door opened, and Mr. McCall leaned out. "Miss Stevens, you can come back in now."

And as Simone rose to meet her fate, she prayed that she was strong enough to handle it. Because whatever happened, it was now out of her hands.

CHANCE CHECKED HIS watch for the thousandth time and asked himself where in the hell she was. Surely by now they had given her the verdict. She had promised to come by when she heard, but still there was no word from her.

He leaned across the litter of puppies nursing at Spooner's nipples and straightened the red bow he had tied around the oldest one's neck. Idly he checked beneath it, to the surprise he had bought this morning—the surprise he had hidden beneath the puppy's fat neck.

Now he wondered if he had lost his mind, thinking Simone would be in any mood to play with puppies and confront surprises today. If she lost her job, which he feared now she had, she might just be so upset that she wouldn't come to be with him at all.

And what did that say for her feelings for him? If she loved him, wouldn't she want to lean on him when she was hurting? Wouldn't she want him to take some of the burden? Wouldn't she need his comfort?

Instead, he feared that she was crawling into a cocoon, that she would withdraw from him, and that it was the beginning of their end.

He heard a car in the drive and quickly dashed out of the barn. Relief flooded his heart as he saw her van pulling to a halt behind his car. Slowly he started toward her.

He couldn't tell from her posture as she got out if she was defeated or victorious. She started walking toward him, her step growing more and more rapid, and suddenly she was running.

She threw her arms around him before he had the chance to determine if it was joy or pain he saw on her face, and he whispered, "I thought you weren't coming! I thought you'd gone home."

"It was a long meeting," she said, and he felt her tears against his neck. "But they're keeping me, Chance! They're not going to fire me!"

He lifted her up then and swung her around, and together they laughed aloud, their voices lilting on the wind. "I knew it!" he said. "I knew they wouldn't let you go!"

"Mrs. Seal got all furious and stormed out, and one of the school-board members said that they should send her a watch or something—like they do when you retire—and Mr. McCall suggested they send my brother's stripper to her house, and the whole board cracked up!"

Chance grinned at her, his own eyes misting, as she rambled on.

"And then they spent the next hour picking my brain about my teaching methods and asking for suggestions about how they could incorporate them into all of the classes in the school! Can you believe it? They were so impressed with my students' test results, that now I'm some kind of hero. Oh, Chance, you should have been there."

"I wanted to," he said, touching her face and not believing how happy and animated it suddenly was, after days of sadness. It was as carefree as it had been the first time he had met her, before her life had threatened to come tumbling down. "But you wouldn't let me."

"I was scared. I didn't want you to see me fail."

"You couldn't have failed even if they'd fired you," he said. "It's just not in you. And you want to know how sure I am about that?"

She nodded and he took her hand, and pulled her into the barn. "I got you a surprise," he whispered, sitting down beside the litter of puppies, and scooping up the one with the bow around its neck.

She caught her breath and took it. "The first one. I recognize the spot on his head. The one I named Gorbachev! Chance, are you giving him to me?"

"If you want him."

"But Dino would eat him. I could never leave them alone together."

"It's all right," he said, his voice dropping to a careful pitch. "You can keep him here."

She brought the puppy to her face, and stroked him along his silky coat. "But if he's mine, I hate not having him with me—" she stopped midsentence as she noticed a small box tied to the bow. "What's this?"

"I don't know," Chance said with a poignant, apprehensive look on his face. "Why don't you open it and see?"

Her smile faded, and she brought her eyes up to his. "All right." Her hands trembled as she untied the little box.

She opened it, and stared down at the brilliant white diamond ring. Her eyes filled with tears as she brought them back to Chance. "What's this?"

As serious as the tears in her eyes, Chance leaned over and took her left hand, slipped the ring out of the box, and whispered, "It's an expression of my love for you, Simone, because words just aren't enough. And it's my way of asking you if you'll marry me."

He slipped the ring on her finger, and she stared down at it, suddenly dizzy, suddenly speechless, suddenly as deliriously happy as she had ever imagined being in her life.

"Oh, Chance... Yes, yes, I'll marry you!"

She threw her arms around him, and he held her as his own tears began to crowd his eyes, tears of relief and joy and hope and anticipation.

The barn door opened and they looked up to see Jeanie and Brian coming in. But there seemed no need to pull apart this time. It was right, their holding each other.

"She didn't get fired!" Brian said, when he saw the smiles on their faces. "All right, Sis! Way to go!"

"Could you two wait outside for a little while?" Chance asked. "We'll come tell you all about it later. Right now, we're busy getting engaged."

"Engaged!" Jeanie blurted out. "You mean like in marriage?"

"Yeah," Simone said, focusing on Chance's face, and realizing it was the most beautiful sight she'd ever seen.

"Wow. Does that mean I'll be Jeanie's step-uncle?" Brian asked. "Will it be illegal for us to date?"

"It's not illegal," Jeanie teased. "We just won't ever be able to have children."

They guffawed against each other, and Chance shot them an impatient look. "I don't know about illegal, but if you two don't get out of here for a few minutes, it could get dangerous."

"Ooops, that sounds like a threat," Brian said. "See you around, guys." He took Jeanie's arm, and pulled her to the door. "See, Jeanie, I told you your father always knows best."

"Gosh," Jeanie said. "Marriage. That's like forever."

And as the door closed behind them, Simone looked up at Chance and touched his face with unleashed adoration...and unfrightened love. "Just like forever," she whispered.

He smiled and held her tighter, as if he would never let her go. "Forever and then some," he said.

And for the first time in her life, Simone truly believed it.

"GET AWAY FROM IT ALL" SWEEPSTAKES

HERE'S HOW THE SWEEPSTAKES WORKS

NO PURCHASE NECESSARY

To enter each drawing, complete the appropriate Official Entry Form or a 3" by 5" index card by hand-printing your name, address and phone number and the trip destination that the entry is being submitted for (i.e., Caneel Bay, Canyon Ranch or London and the English Countryside) and mailing it to: Get Away From It All Sweepstakes, P.O. Box 1397, Buffalo, New York 14269-1397.

No responsibility is assumed for lost, late or misdirected mail. Entries must be sent separately with first class postage affixed, and be received by: 4/15/92 for the Caneel Bay Vacation Drawing, 5/15/92 for the Canyon Ranch Vacation Drawing and 6/15/92 for the London and the English Countryside Vacation Drawing. Sweepstakes is open to residents of the U.S. (except Puerto Rico) and Canada, 21 years of age or older as of 5/31/92.

For complete rules send a self-addressed, stamped (WA residents need not affix return postage) envelope to: Get Away From It All Sweepstakes, P.O. Box 4892, Blair, NE 68009.

"GET AWAY FROM IT ALL" SWEEPSTAKES

HERE'S HOW THE SWEEPSTAKES WORKS

NO PURCHASE NECESSARY

To enter each drawing, complete the appropriate Official Entry Form or a 3" by 5" index card by hand-printing your name, address and phone number and the trip destination that the entry is being submitted for (i.e., Caneel Bay, Canyon Ranch or London and the English Countryside) and mailing it to: Get Away From It All Sweepstakes, P.O. Box 1397, Buffalo, New York 14269-1397.

No responsibility is assumed for lost, late or misdirected mail. Entries must be sent separately with first class postage affixed, and be received by: 4/15/92 for the Caneel Bay Vacation Drawing, 5/15/92 for the Canyon Ranch Vacation Drawing and 6/15/92 for the London and the English Countryside Vacation Drawing. Sweepstakes is open to residents of the U.S. (except Puerto Rico) and Canada, 21 years of age or older as of 5/31/92.

For complete rules send a self-addressed, stamped (WA residents need not affix return postage) envelope to: Get Away From It All Sweepstakes, P.O. Box 4892, Blair, NE 68009.

© 1992 HARLEQUIN ENTERPRISES LTD. SWP-RLS

"GET AWAY FROM IT ALL"

Brand-new Subscribers-Only Sweepstakes

OFFICIAL ENTRY FORM

This entry must be received by: May 15, 1992
This month's winner will be notified by: May 31, 1992
Trip must be taken between: June 30, 1992—June 30, 1993

YES, I want to win the Canyon Ranch vacation for two. I understand the prize includes round-trip airfare and the two additional prizes revealed in the BONUS PRIZES insert.

Name ______________________________

Address ______________________________

City ______________________________

State/Prov. ______________ Zip/Postal Code ______________

Daytime phone number ______________________________
(Area Code)

Return entries with invoice in envelope provided. Each book in this shipment has two entry coupons — and the more coupons you enter, the better your chances of winning!

 2M-CPN

"GET AWAY FROM IT ALL"

Brand-new Subscribers-Only Sweepstakes

OFFICIAL ENTRY FORM

This entry must be received by: May 15, 1992
This month's winner will be notified by: May 31, 1992
Trip must be taken between: June 30, 1992—June 30, 1993

YES, I want to win the Canyon Ranch vacation for two. I understand the prize includes round-trip airfare and the two additional prizes revealed in the BONUS PRIZES insert.

Name ______________________________

Address ______________________________

City ______________________________

State/Prov. ______________ Zip/Postal Code ______________

Daytime phone number ______________________________
(Area Code)

Return entries with invoice in envelope provided. Each book in this shipment has two entry coupons — and the more coupons you enter, the better your chances of winning!

© 1992 HARLEQUIN ENTERPRISES LTD. 2M-CPN